Omensford Series – Book 4

# Pumpkins & Popstars

G Clatworthy

ISBN: 978-1-915516-23-7

# Foreword

The Omensford witches first arrived in my writing in <u>Attack on Avalon</u> (book 5 in the Rise of the Dragons series), but they were too interesting to leave there so they had to have their own book. And so, this series was born, based around the fictional town of Omensford in the Cotswolds and the witches who live there. Cirian, the elven popstar from the Rise of the Dragons series, and Dot's crush, also makes an appearance in this book – he's the popstar in the title, always stealing the show.

A special thank you to my amazing typo hunters, grammar gurus, and plot pickers who got this story to where it is today. You are awesome!

If you want to support Gemma, you can find her on <u>www.patreon.com/G_Clatworthy</u> for exclusive first reads of new stories. You can also join her newsletter at <u>www.gemmaclatworthy.com</u> for a free short story based on one of the witches in the Omensford series and follow Gemma on <u>www.instagram.com/gemmaclatworthy</u>, <u>www.facebook.com/gemmaclatworthy</u> or join the reader's group on Facebook: <u>Gemma's book wyrms.</u>

# Chapter 1

Fi stood up and wiped the mud from her hands.

"Do you see it?" Harris shifted his stance, his wellies making sucking noises as he moved in the inch-deep mud.

Fi sighed. "Maybe it's some sort of track but it looks a lot like the ridges your tractor makes, Harris…"

"Then where are the treads? I'm tellin' you it's no tractor. I would of heard something."

"I'll check the 'tracks' against the Magical Liaison Office database." Fi took out her phone and snapped some pictures of the deep marks in the ground.

"And what am I going to do? Halloween's coming up and I haven't got a single pumpkin to take to St Columba's for the Tri-Village Fete. Thank goodness they didn't take my carrot, or I wouldn't have a shot at most humorous vegetable in show. 'Ere, do you want a look? I've got it back at the house…"

"Maybe later." Fi shook off the mental image of Harris' carrot. He'd won the most humorous vegetable in show prize five years in a row and his vegetables were always anatomically shaped. Last year's was…she flushed with embarrassment even thinking about it. She tuned back into the present.

Harris leaned more heavily on the staff as he looked over the dark ground. Fi reached out an arm to pat him on the shoulder, a pang of sympathy for the old warlock trumping her natural dislike of feelings. She surveyed the empty field again. Harris assured her that yesterday it had been teeming with row upon row of pumpkins of every size and colour, but this morning, only the green vines remained. It was weird. Pumpkins didn't just get up and walk off. The police had suspected magic, or so Detective Ledd had said when he'd called and asked her to trek out to Harris' farm.

His exact words when he'd palmed the case off on her had been "That old warlock has probably conjured a vanishing spell in his sleep, sounds like supernatural shenanigans to me. You go and reassure him."

So, here she was as the Cotswolds Magical Liaison Office community agent, investigating the mystery of the missing pumpkins. She stopped the snort that threatened to leave her nose. Not exactly the big case that she wanted.

A small patch of gold moved towards them, flashing in the weak sunlight.

"Did you find anything?" Fi asked her familiar.

*You're going to want to see this.*

Fi frowned down at Cressida. It was unlike the dragon-like creature to play games. "What is it?"

*This way.*

Fi took a step forward and then grimaced as the small wyrm clambered up her beige trench coat, smearing mud all over it. "Hey!"

*If you think I am traipsing back through that quagmire, you have another think coming.*

"Fine." Fi's frown deepened but her coat was already covered with mud, so she allowed the wyrm to stay draped around her shoulders.

Fi followed the wyrm's directions down the field and Harris hobbled along behind them, his staff squelching an accompaniment to their steps.

*Down there.* Cressida nodded towards a ditch at the edge of the field.

Fi stepped over the bank and froze. There, lying face down in the pooled water of the drainage ditch was a body.

She motioned for Harris to stay back, but it was too late.

"Nigel!" He sank to the ground, not seeming to feel the cold mud seeping through his work overalls.

Fi let him wail for a minute while she took pictures for evidence, and then she tapped her hand against her thigh awkwardly as Harris continued to sob. When she thought he was over the initial emotional outburst at seeing the body, she linked her hand under his elbow and helped him up.

He whirled to face the witch. "I knew there was something amiss here, and see, the same tracks!" He pointed to the ground and Fi nodded and snapped some more photos on her phone.

Fi asked him to head back to his house, then made a call.

"What is it? Did he remember he'd picked his pumpkins already?" Detective Ledd laughed at his own poor joke.

"No. You're going to want to come down here. There's a dead body."

"Dead?" The detective's voice sharpened. "Are you sure?"

Fi nodded and swallowed. "Pretty sure. He's missing a head."

# Chapter 2

Fi brewed Harris a cup of tea back at the farmhouse as they waited for the police to finish their crime scene analysis. The old farmer was in shock at the loss of his trusted foreman, but the promise of a strong cuppa and the chance to show Fi his knobbly carrot had helped. She was still recovering from the shock of the root vegetable.

Detective Ledd stamped the mud from his wellies as he came in the back door. Fi looked up. He shook his head.

"We've got the scene taped off and the ambulance is on the way for the body. I'm not sure how we'll get it over the field though…" He trailed off.

"No problem, I'll use the tractor. Not like I need to worry about squashing any pumpkins now."

"Thank you for the offer, but…"

Harris stood and banged on the worn tabletop. "I want to help. Better than sittin' 'ere and moping around. Nigel was like family to me, and he'd like to have one final ride on the trailer." With that Harris walked out.

The detective scratched his bald spot and exhaled loudly. His eyes paused on the humongous vegetable lying on the table. Fi could almost see him deciding whether he could charge a carrot with public indecency. Instead, he ignored it. "What do you make of it?"

Fi shrugged. "It's odd. I mean, why take the head? Harris knew who it was straight away thanks to his clothes. No one else wore an orange shirt that bright."

"Do you think it was a ritual?"

"Not everything is magical."

"I know." Larry Ledd held up his hands in a gesture of contrition. "But the scene of crime folk say that the head was ripped off. Who could do that? What could do that?"

Fi shuddered. "Is that what killed him?"

The detective nodded. "Looks like. We'll know more tomorrow at the autopsy. Horrible way to go. You don't think a werewolf…"

"Don't even finish that sentence."

"Fine," the detective huffed. "But there's something supernatural going on here, so I need you to be objective."

"I am objective, but I want proof if you're going to start accusing my friends."

Larry pulled out his leatherbound notebook and turned back a couple of pages. "He is, was, a good fella. I doubt anyone would have a bad word to say about him." Fi rolled her eyes as he brushed past their disagreement about the latent tendencies of supernaturals. "Your, er, familiar didn't smell anything did she?"

*At last, he thinks to ask me.*

"Did you smell anything?" Fi repeated the question.

*Only pumpkins, blood, and your electricity.*

Fi relayed the message then turned back to the wyrm. "What do you mean my electricity?" She hadn't accidentally used her magic in the field, had she?

If a reptile could shrug, Fi thought Cressida would have done so. Instead, she just gave the witch a look.

*I only know what I smelled, and it smells like your magic.*

"Thanks, that's really helpful."

The detective shot Fi a questioning look at her sarcasm, so she clarified, "Cressida didn't smell anything out of the ordinary."

A tractor engine roared to life outside. Detective Ledd glanced out of the window. "I'd better go and help. I'll be in touch when I've got the autopsy time."

Fi nodded and opened her mouth to reply when the cheerful bleep of her phone's text message alert interrupted her thoughts.

*Café emergency! Come as quick as you can!*

Chapter 3

Fi burst into the café.

"What is it? What's happened?"

Steve held up two napkins. "I can't decide whether to go for the swans or the crowns."

Fi leant against the wall, panting hard. "This is your emergency? I ran here from Harris' farm. In wellies."

*I keep saying you need a better exercise regime.*

Fi made a face at her familiar and glared at the werewolf as he sheepishly put down the neatly folded origami serviettes.

"Coffee?" he asked. "I've just assembled the machine, you can be my test subject."

Fi nodded. "And a water." She moved to a chair as Steve placed a glass of tap water on the table and then coaxed the new machine into making a black coffee. It made strange bubbling noises, vibrated and then shot out a jet of steam that missed Steve by the width of her gaming mouse, that is, by not very much.

"Er, I'll use the instant coffee."

He boiled a kettle and soon had two cups of coffee on the table. Fi ignored his looks as her muddy coat grazed the dust sheet covering the chair, closed her eyes and drank deeply, allowing the rich aroma of the beans to transport her to a place of peace. The deep, bitter scent filled the café and nearly masked the fresh paint smell.

"I used the Goblin Blend."

"Thanks." Fi took a sip. "But next time, just send me a picture of the bloody napkins."

Steve smiled brightly. "Well, now that you're here…"

Fi held up a hand. "Let me finish my coffee first." She drank slowly, savouring the taste as she looked around the room. Steve had transformed Effie's café into a light, airy space, perfect for the tourists who came to Omensford for an authentic magical experience.

The second she put down her mug, Steve held up a postcard and placed it in front of her. "This came today."

Fi leant forward and read aloud.


*You're doing a fabulous job with our café. Everything is going to plan. I'm on my way to pick up Cirian in London and bring him back to our village. Fi – look to your past to solve your current case, and please have it all tied up before the opening. Love Effie x*

*PS Steve, don't worry about the crystal ball.*

She turned it over and smiled at the picture of the French chateau on the back. Effie had travelled around most of Western Europe over the past few months. Fi didn't wonder how she knew about the case; Effie was a psychic and had a habit of leaving cryptic messages. Fi hoped that meant she could solve the murder quickly.

"What do you think she means 'Don't worry about the crystal ball'? I was going to recreate her reading room at the back for psychic consultations, but maybe she doesn't want that…" Steve's face creased with worry, and he reached into a packing box to pull out a large crystal ball. He held it in one hand and regarded its semi-opaque surface.

The bell above the door rang as Glen pushed it open. Steve winced at the sound and the ball rolled out of his hand. He reached for it and flicked it up, once, twice, before it hit the floor.

Fi watched with an open mouth as the crystal bounced and rolled away. They breathed out simultaneous sighs of relief.

The crystal travelled over the freshly polished floor until it hit the wall, whereupon it smashed.

Steve groaned and Fi raised an eyebrow. Effie had proved her psychic powers once again.

*That bell's a bit loud.*

"Stating the obvious, Cress."

*Don't call me Cress.*

"How's my entrepreneurial husband today?" asked Glen, crossing the room to give his husband a hug.

Steve's shoulders drooped. "Hardly an entrepreneur. Effie owns the place." He walked over to the counter and retrieved a dustpan and brush.

Glen shot Fi a questioning look as Steve swept up the shards. Fi shrugged. Steve's emotions had been running high ever since Effie had asked him to get the place ready.

"I brought muffins." Glen held up a brown bag.

Steve dumped the broken glass into a binbag and sat down at the table. He slumped in his seat. "This place is never going to be ready before Halloween."

Fi took a triple chocolate muffin, peeling back the paper casing and picking off a chunk to eat. Sugar made everything better.

"Of course, it will. We'll all help. What can we do?"

Steve brightened up. "Well..."

# Chapter 4

Fi placed the box carefully on the floor and wiped the sweat from her forehead. Crystals and wands were heavy. At least this was the last box. Steve had decided on a maximalist approach to stocking the shelves at the back of the café with magical knick-knacks. Fi ripped through the packing tape and picked up a skull made from some sort of green stone.

She shook her head as she placed it high up in the display. She never understood why people wanted all this stuff, it wasn't like it made you better at magic, at least, not in her experience.

The witch took out a bag of dark stones with flashes of amber layered through them. Her lips lifted in a half smile, and she removed a couple from their bag, enjoying the smooth feel of the warm stones against her palm. She remembered collecting tiger's eye stones as a teenager to try to help her control her power, but nothing had worked.

She placed the gems into a see-through plastic box on one of the shelves and turned to the next bag.

Steve bustled over. "Great work!" He took the jade skull from its spot, moved it three inches to the left and angled it towards the door.

Fi rolled her eyes and carried on tipping stones into plastic boxes. They rattled pleasantly as they filled the tubs.

"I can't do any more on the mural today, it needs to dry. So, all that's left are the labels, and the cutlery, and the napkins, and the storeroom." He put his head in his hands. "We're never going to finish in time."

Fi looked around for help as he started to blubber. Glen had made his excuses and gone back to his antique shop to deal with a 'polishing emergency' after Steve had asked him to rearrange the tables for the third time. She patted him on the arm.

"It's been a long day. You're just tired. We all are. Let's call it a night and come back tomorrow."

Steve nodded, his hazel eyes filled with tears. "You're right," he sniffed.

"Of course, I am. It looks great and Effie's going to love it. Why don't you go home and have a night off with Glen and Zadie?"

At the mention of his daughter, Steve's eyes lit up. "That's exactly what I need. I've been so distracted getting everything ready that I've barely cooked this week. Last night, Glen told me he'd bought frozen fishfingers for dinner." The werewolf shuddered.

Fi stood and followed him out, retrieving her muddy coat from the stand next to the door.

"Oh, I nearly forgot." Steve dashed back inside. He returned with a pile of painted pumpkins. "Here, we want to get into the Halloween spirit." He handed Fi a white one with the word 'Boo' scrawled across it in neat calligraphy, before setting his own pumpkins in an artful display next to the door.

"You sure you want to leave them outside? What about teenagers?"

Steve scoffed. "Who's going to take a bunch of pumpkins? See you tomorrow."

The werewolf trotted down the hill to his house. Fi felt a pang of envy. She missed having Glen and Steve for neighbours – Zadie she could do without – she suppressed a sigh as she allowed Cressida to climb onto her shoulders. There were benefits to being back home with her mother; no rent, for example, and her mum's cooking. She tried to think of some more.

Fi's phone buzzed with a familiar song, causing her to smile. She put the pumpkin down, answered her phone and began to walk back home.

"Hi."

"Hi yourself." Fi's stomach lurched at the sound of the doctor's deep voice. "Are we still on for tomorrow night?"

"Yep."

He must have sensed her slight pause. "Hey, if you don't want to go to a haunted house, we can pick somewhere else for our date."

Fi ran her hands through her long hair, enjoying the rush of warmth that flooded through her stomach when he said 'date'.

It still amazed her that they were going out. She thought for a second; yes, she would prefer to stay in and play videogames, but they'd done that the last few times they'd had alone time, and how many more times could she kick his ass at Mario Kart or vintage Street Fighter or…well, pretty much any game they played that wasn't co-operative, without his ego getting permanently bruised? "No, I'm good. Really. Pick me up at eight?"

"Great, see you tomorrow, and don't worry, I'll protect you."

"More like I'll protect you."

They both laughed and Fi ended the call. She had no doubt he could protect her, he had some sort of power connected to death and a sword that he knew how to handle, if they let weapons into a haunted house. But she wasn't exactly a helpless maiden. Her electrical powers swirled under her skin, and she allowed a little to trickle out onto her fingertips, breathing slowly to control the magic.

*Are you quite finished?* Cressida asked from her perch, wriggling and interrupting Fi's tight concentration over her magic. *I need a proper bath, not just a rinse under the tap.*

Fi's bolt of electricity collided with a streetlamp, causing a shower of sparks to erupt from the light. Passers-by stopped to stare.

"Bloody council," Fi said to no one in particular as she hurried home.

# Chapter 5

Fi kicked up a pile of dried, crisp autumn leaves to the side of the garden path, caught by a spontaneous rush of joy. She had a date. With a man who enjoyed her company.

Fi smiled up at the twirling leaves, laughing as they slipped through her fingers on a gust of wind. She slid through the mud with the grace of an ice skater, thrilling in the feeling of happiness and freedom.

Fi's skid came to a stop near a grey donkey munching on long grass at the end of the garden. She reached out to pet him. Before she could touch his velvety ears, the ass snapped his head round and bit down in the spot where her fingers would have been if she hadn't snatched them away.

"Feeling a bit temperamental today, are we?"

The donkey turned his back on her and the muscles in his hind legs bunched. Fi hurried up the path, out of range of his powerful legs. She stuck out her tongue at his back from the safety of the porch.

She took a breath and thought about him more charitably. It couldn't be easy for the demon, Timaeus, to be stuck as an ass. She tilted her head to one side. Of course, he had been an ass before, when he'd tried to open a gateway to the demon realm and forced his disciple to kill people so he could drain their life essence, leaving desiccated corpses in his wake, but now he was a donkey. Fi still didn't understand exactly how that had happened. But she was in a good mood after speaking to the doctor and an encounter with a demon donkey wasn't going to change that.

The house opened the back door as she approached, and she gave it an affectionate pat on the doorframe as she passed through. The doormat flapped on the tiles in front of her, and she took the hint, wiping her wellies and placing them on the boot rack just inside the door.

Her niece sat at the kitchen table colouring. "Aunty Fi!"

"Bumble Bea!" Fi bent over and wrapped her arms around the girl, before scruffing her hair playfully.

Her mother and sister stopped fussing over the pots on the stove to look at Fi.

"You're in a good mood."

"Can't I be happy?" Fi reverted to sullen teenager at her mum's observation.

"It's nice to see."

Slightly mollified, Fi took a step towards the kitchen. "Need a hand?"

They both shook their heads in tandem and her mother held up a spatula in warning. "You stay right over there until you're out of those muddy clothes."

Fi motioned for Cressida to jump down and hung up her mud-smeared coat. She grimaced. That coat was dry clean only.

"So why are you so happy then? Has it got anything to do with Dr dreamboat?" Agatha teased.

Fi blushed.

"I knew it! Where's he taking you?"

"The haunted house at the farm."

"I went there with Liv at the weekend, I screamed so hard I peed myself a little."

"Agatha! Really," Nell admonished her daughter.

Agatha shrugged. "I'm serious. Do your pelvic floor exercises before you go."

Fi shook her head and backed out of the cooking space to join her niece at the table. An elegant young lady entered. Fi jumped up, shocked by the appearance of the woman who'd tried to kill her. It took Fi a minute to recognise her friend's sparkling eyes above the sequined dress, and she relaxed.

But then she'd known Effie as an old woman for years. It was only last year that the nonagenarian had taken on this younger body – the one that her homicidal sister had literally killed for – and used her new lease of life to travel around Europe.

"Effie!" She rushed over and gave the witch a hug. "How was France? And Italy? And…"

Effie held up a manicured hand and glided over to take a seat at the table. "It was a dream."

An elf ducked through the door after her, stealing the attention from Effie. The entire Blair family turned to look at him, then stared. He was gorgeous. He smiled and Fi's heart fluttered at the small dimple in his cheek. Logically, she knew it was only elven glamour, but her brain overrode that and melted, rendering her speechless at his beauty.

"Cirian, meet my oldest friend Nell and her two daughters, Agatha and Fiona, and of course, her granddaughter, Bea. Everyone, meet Cirian." Effie spoke and broke the spell.

"The popstar?"

He waved off the title. "I just love music and people like to hear me perform."

"So how did you two meet?" Nell was the first to recover. Fi elbowed Agatha and her sister shut her mouth.

"You have a husband," Fi mouthed, and Agatha shrugged, keeping her gaze on the elf's perfect face.

Cirian patted Effie's hand. "Oh, we met many years ago."

"I was a fashion consultant in Breconia when I first saw him, but we've kept in touch." She smiled up at the tall elf. "How's the case going?"

Fi opened her mouth to answer, but a reptilian voice sounded in her head.

*If you've quite finished, perhaps you could see to my bath.*

"Sorry, I'd better go clean this one up."

*This one?!*

Fi held the door open, and Cressida stalked through it. Fi trailed behind as the wyrm made her way upstairs to the bathroom. Flakes of mud dropped from the animal's golden scales as she walked.

"Make sure you tidy up any mess," her mother called from the kitchen. Fi made a face and Cressida's walk changed.

"Are you deliberately trying to get mud everywhere?" Fi narrowed her eyes at the wyrm.

*No. Whyever would you think that?*

Cressida's innocent tone didn't fool Fi as the wyrm's tail brushed against the patterned wallpaper in the hall. Fi didn't respond. It would only make the wyrm more contrary and, no doubt, lead to more work for her. Instead, she followed her familiar into the family bathroom and turned on the hot tap to fill the clawfoot bath. Cressida sat on the white bathmat and then lay down. Was she trying to rub the dirt in?

"Could you not?"

*Pardon?*

"Could you stop acting like a brat? Familiars are meant to help their witches, not cause them more work."

*I do help you. Who found that body earlier?*

"Whatever." Urg, now she sounded like a teenager again. "Do you want bubbles?"

Cressida hopped onto the side of the bath and sniffed the bottles of bubble bath. *That one.*

Fi unscrewed the cap on the eucalyptus bottle, holding it away from her nose. It was pungent. She swirled in some of the thick green liquid. "Ouch! That'll boil you."

*I like it hot.*

Fi shrugged and turned off the water. Cressida jumped in, splashing the witch with bubbles and too hot water. Fi frowned down at the wyrm, but she couldn't keep a straight face. The small reptile looked so happy frolicking in the bath and blowing bubbles that Fi had to smile. It was almost worth the annoyance of having to clean up after her. Almost.

# Chapter 6

Fi ran down the stairs to the kitchen and grabbed a piece of toast from the toast rack.

"That's for our guests!" Her mother reprimanded.

"Sorry. I'm late. Cress, are you coming down or not?" The wyrm looked up at Fi from where she sat next to the door. "Oh, good. You're here. I don't want you trapped upstairs again."

*Neither do I. I still have nightmares about being crushed by a pile of dirty washing.*

"Just stay out of trouble while I'm gone."

*I'm not the one who gets into trouble.*

"I don't suppose I could get some of that coffee?" Fi ignored her familiar and blinked pleading eyes at her mother. Nell rolled her own blue eyes, but she poured out a cup from the pot that she'd brewed.

"Thank you, you're a lifesaver."

"Really Fi, it's only coffee. Maybe you should cut back a bit?"

"I'm going to pretend you didn't say that," Fi shot back as she pulled on her converse trainers and coat. The mud had now dried into a thin crust over the beige fabric.

"That bathmat still needs a wash."

"Sorry, Mum, got to go. Coroner's waiting. I'll sort it later." Toast in one hand and travel mug in the other, she raced out of the door.

*Please don't have left. Please don't have left.* Fi chanted the refrain inside her head to the beat of her feet hitting the pavement. She got to the bus stop in time to see the number forty-two bus pull away.

"No!" She waved but it kept going. Fi panted and bent over to ease the stitch in her side. She swore in between gasps of air. The autopsy was at ten o' clock. She'd have to ask for a lift. The witch pulled out her phone and called her sister.

"Fi? Are you alright? I'm about to start my class."

"Oh, yeah, no I was calling about a lift…" Fi left the sentence hanging, hoping that her sister's overwhelming need to help people would compel Agatha to come to her aid.

"Sorry, any other time, but I'm at work today." Fi heard the cacophony of school children in the background. "Look, I've got to go, they're ringing the bell. Good luck."

Fi swore again. Her powers tingled under her skin, threatening to erupt. She damped them down. She did not need to destroy another phone. Fi considered her options and decided to ask her mum. She tramped back to the house and found her mother laughing with Effie in the guest dining room of the Bed & Breakfast.

"So how did you get Cirian to perform at your café opening? Kathryn said he only does stadium gigs nowadays."

Effie's laugh trilled across the room. She leant forward, ready to impart top secret knowledge about her and Cirian's relationship, and then paused. "Fi."

"Fi?" Nell turned. "Fi! What are you doing here?"

"I missed the bus. I don't suppose you could take me to the coroner's office?"

"Sorry dear, I've got a busy day ahead. I promised Effie I'd go with her to look at the café and I've got jobs to do round the house, not to mention the WWWI agenda for October's meeting needs looking at. Honestly, this place goes crazy at Halloween."

Fi groaned. Bloody Witches', Wizards', and Warlocks' Institute. Yes, her mother was the Chairwoman, but was it really more important than her youngest daughter?

"Fine, I'll make my own way there." Fi marched to the cupboard under the stairs and retrieved her state-of-the-art vacuum cleaner from behind a feather duster.

"Wait a minute, I need that. I was going to hoover upstairs."

"Sorry, Mum, gotta go." Fi was already at the door.

She pressed the on switch and allowed her magic to flow into the machine; a Suxor Platinum X-5000 that promised the suction power of a tornado.

It purred to life and the battery display flashed as it drew on her electrical magic. Fi swung her leg over the thin nozzle attachment and kicked off.

# Chapter 7

Fi landed on the gravelled drive outside the morgue with a loud crunch next to the detective's small car. She turned off the vacuum cleaner and noted the small stones in the chamber with a sigh – she'd have to empty that before she went home. Lifting the X-5000, she jogged over to the glass doors.

The receptionist looked up with a welcoming, yet sombre, smile that fit the mood of the morgue down to a tee. Then she blinked rapidly at the dust-covered newcomer.

"Can I help you?"

"I'm here for the autopsy. The headless body."

The receptionist swallowed and asked for an ID badge before gesturing down the hall. "Examination room one."

Fi took a step in that direction before turning back. "Can I, er, leave this here with you while I'm in the room?"

The receptionist took the proffered vacuum with her fingertips as if she was afraid of it and placed it behind the desk. Fi smiled, trying to put the woman at ease, but it didn't seem to work. She gave up and hurried to the examination room, slipping off her coat along the way.

She paused at the door and peeked in through the small glass pane. The body was covered by a sheet, but Fi still shuddered with apprehension; dead bodies were her least favourite part of the job. Even worse than talking to the community.

She took a breath of the lemon scented air. It had the tang of strong disinfectant under it, but below that was a base note of decay. Steeling her shoulders, she entered the room.

Detective Ledd and Robbie, the coroner, looked up. And then stared at the witch.

"Bit windy out?" asked Robbie.

Larry was more direct. "Someone drag you through a bush backwards, Blair?"

Fi's eyebrows drew together, and she checked her reflection in one of the polished metal surfaces. She let out a yelp of surprise. Her white hair was out of control, whipped up around her head like a bird's nest. No wonder pictures always showed witches wearing hats when they rode brooms; if they didn't, they'd end up looking like a crazy hedgehog. Her hair almost had as much volume as when she used too much of her power and it stuck out like a cartoon image of someone being electrocuted.

"What's the plan?" she asked, flattening down the mess as much as she could and tying it back in a frizzy ponytail.

The detective raised his bushy eyebrows at her. "We get the autopsy done. We were waiting for you."

"Well, I'm here now."

"No need to get snippy with me, young lady. Are you prepared? I don't want you fainting or anything."

Fi could feel her power swirling inside her, rising to the surface in response to the detective's needling comment. She opened her mouth, but Robbie interrupted by knocking her knuckles on the metal operating slab.

"If you've quite finished? I've got a day full of corpses ahead of me, so I'd like to crack on, if it's alright with you two."

"Sorry, Robbie. Please," Larry gestured at the sheet.

"Yeah, sorry," Fi mumbled.

"OK, I took a quick look earlier but let's go through the motions," said the coroner, folding back the crisp white sheet. "We've got a fifty-one-year-old male identified as Nigel Burns, but we're unable to verify using dental records due to the body having no head. I'll take a sample for DNA matching to his closest family after the autopsy. Time of death estimated at around eleven thirty the night before he was found..."

"Harris said he offered to stay the night in the stables to keep old Jessie company. He said the horse was suffering from..." Larry consulted his notebook, "...colic and needed supervision. The vet arrived at about ten p.m. and Nigel left to check out a noise in the fields about eleven. He never came back."

"Didn't the vet think something might have happened to him?" Fi couldn't stop herself from asking.

The detective lowered his black eyebrows and flicked through a couple of pages. "Nope. He said he thought Nigel might have gone to look at the cow that had diarrhoea and stayed with her. And the vet was preoccupied with the horse; he stayed through the night and the horse was doing well when he left at six a.m."

Fi was impressed. The detective had done a lot of work while she had been faffing about in a café with Steve.

Robbie bent over the neck. Fi swallowed hard, her throat clamming up. She focused on one of the cabinets and told herself to breathe and imagine it was one of the corpses in the videogames she played. Some of them were graphic, but, she sneaked a look back at the naked corpse, none of the games compared with the reality of seeing a dead body. She glanced to the side; even the self-proclaimed hardened detective looked a bit green.

"Interesting…there's a lot of bruising around the neck. I'd say the deceased was strangled before being decapitated. Looks like the blood congealed here rather than the spray I'd expect to see if they'd cut off his head while he was alive."

"There was blood on the ground…" Fi started.

"I'm sure, but I saw the crime scene photographs. There just isn't enough for him to have been alive first. Just as well really. The edge of the neck is jagged, could have been sawn off, but…"

"But?"

"But I can't see any blade marks on the spinal column, it's like it popped at vertebrae C3 or 4." She looked up, her glasses gleaming under the harsh electric lighting. "Almost like his head was ripped off."

"How much force would that take?" Larry had his notebook out, pencil poised.

"No idea, but it takes a lot to dislocate a bone. And to tear through the spine as well as all the muscle in the neck…a lot."

The detective closed his book. Fi pulled out her phone and looked it up. "Five hundred newtons." They both looked at her and Fi put her phone away. "That's what it says on Reddit anyway, if you can believe an internet forum."

"Why were they asking?" Larry's eyebrows drew together in puzzlement.

"I'm not going down that rabbit hole."

The coroner coughed. "Back to the facts. There's bruising around his arms, legs and torso too. See this?" Robbie pointed to a ring of purplish skin around his arm. "I'd say something restrained him with extreme force."

"Like ropes?" Fi asked.

"Perhaps…but it's more like the bruising you see in domestic abuse cases, where the victim is held down and forcibly restrained. Although, the size of the hand you'd need to get round the upper arm." Robbie demonstrated with her own squat fingers and Detective Ledd moved over to try his.

"Whoever it was had large hands. Supernaturally large." Larry shot Fi a look that said 'I told you so' as he jotted that gem of wisdom down in his notebook.

"Taking samples from under the nails now." Robbie scraped at the dirty fingernails. "There's nothing obvious, but the lab might find something in all that muck." She deposited the sample into a smallish plastic jar and labelled it in messy capital letters.

"OK, guess I'd better open him up."

# Chapter 8

In the small room that served as a kitchen / relaxation area for the morgue staff, Fi finally felt able to take a deep breath. Robbie handed her a black coffee, with two sugars, and sat down on an offensively orange sofa. Fi shifted on the threadbare seat and took a sip. The coroner had been heavy-handed with the sugar – perfect.

"What do you make of it?" Fi asked as the detective joined them with his own milky tea the colour of a pinecone.

"Hmmm," Robbie tapped a finger against her glasses as she thought. "Honestly, I've got no idea. But in most cases with extreme violence, there's some sort of connection between killer and victim that sets off a deep-seated rage in the killer."

"So, you think Nigel knew his killer?"

"Not necessarily. Nigel could have represented something that stirred the murderer's ire. But with this sort of anger, it's likely that something could set him off again."

"Him?"

Robbie waved a hand dismissively. "Just a figure of speech. Whoever it is, they're strong and capable of decapitating someone with their bare hands." The coroner shuddered. "I wouldn't like to meet them in a dark alley, that's for sure."

Fi took a long drink.

"And what about you?" asked the detective.

"Me?"

"Have you got any leads?"

"Oh, right. I'm still looking into it."

He gave Fi a meaningful look. "Well, let us know if you find anything that would help. And the thing about policework is that you have to be objective, no matter where the facts take you."

Fi arched an eyebrow. That was rich coming from the detective who tried to blame supernaturals for everything. "I'll let you know, but one thing I do know is that it wasn't werewolves."

"How can you be so sure? They're strong enough to do something like this and you have to admit that violence is part of their nature."

"Firstly, the only werewolves round here are some of the nicest people I know. But more importantly, a werewolf has claws and teeth. There were no marks like that on the body." She looked at Robbie, who nodded her agreement. "And why would a werewolf take a head?"

"Why would anyone want the head?" He shot back.

"If the head is missing, I'd normally say the killer doesn't want the police to identify the victim. But, in this case, it didn't work. Are there any magic rituals that require a head?"

"I'm looking into it." Fi kept her face neutral as she drank her coffee, but inside she groaned; working for the Magical Liaison Office was really messing up her search history. She glanced out of the small window and noticed the raindrops studding the glass.

"Are you going to Omensford?" Fi changed the subject, angling for a lift. Travelling by vacuum cleaner was fun for short distances but she hadn't accounted for rain; her coat didn't even have a hood.

Larry shook his head. "Sorry, I'm heading back to the station. You'll let us know if the samples come back with anything interesting?"

"Naturally," Robbie nodded.

They deposited their cups in the sink and walked to the reception. Fi shrugged on her coat.

"Have you been rolling in crap, Blair?" Larry screwed up his face as he eyed her jacket.

Fi looked down at her mud-encrusted coat. "It's just dirt."

"You should think about how you present yourself. You're employed by His Majesty's government. You need to embody all the respect a public office deserves."

"Hey, it got muddy in the line of duty; at Harris' farm."

Detective Ledd snorted.

"Do you want to wash it off?" the coroner asked.

Fi shook her head. "I'll brush it off later."

The receptionist nervously put Fi's vacuum cleaner on her desk and pushed it as far away from her as she could without it falling on the floor.

Larry and Robbie stared at Fi.

"What? It's my mode of transport… if you're sure you're not going past Omensford…"

The detective shook his head. Fi wasn't sure if he was confirming he couldn't give her a ride or if he was too flabbergasted that she travelled via vacuum.

"I've heard of a witch on a broomstick but isn't that going a bit far?" Flabbergasted it was.

She shrugged and followed him outside. Fi paused to empty the chamber of its gravel and squinted up into the cloudy sky. Now she was out here, she wasn't sure it was a good idea to use electrical goods while it was raining. But then, the rain wasn't too heavy, and the only other choice was waiting an hour for a bus. So, not really a choice at all.

Fi waved goodbye to the detective as he got into his car looking a little smug, switched her mount on, and kicked off into the unwelcoming wind.

# Chapter 9

Fi's phone rang while she was over the small mound known locally as Dragon's Hill. She considered answering it, but her hands were chilled into position gripping the purple handle of the X-5000 and she didn't trust herself to answer without falling to her death or dropping her phone. She made a mental note to get some Bluetooth earbuds for use while she was flying.

She landed in her mother's back garden with an ungraceful thud and switched off the vacuum cleaner. The house opened for her, and she tramped inside. She rested the X-5000 against the wall and unlaced her soaking trainers before hanging her coat on a hook. The dusty dirt had re-wettened itself into mud in the rain and her trench coat was soaked through. Fi swore and rubbed her hands together, trying to get some warmth back into her fingers.

Cressida opened one emerald eye and looked up from her spot by the aga cooker.

*What happened to you?*

"What?" Her hand snaked up to her hair and she walked into the hall to check. "It's not that…bad…" She trailed off as she caught sight of herself in the mirror.

*You look like you've had a fight with your hairbrush. And lost.*

"It's fine, I'll just tie it back up." Fi untied her ponytail and fought to smooth down the mess with her fingers. "Where is everyone?"

*They went to see the café.*

"And you didn't go with them?"

*I decided to wait for you.*

"Thanks." Fi meant it. Maybe this was the supportive side of the familiar bond that she kept reading about.

*And it was warm here.*

There it was. "OK, well I'd better go and support Steve." She checked her phone. "He called me twice while I was in the air." She sent him a quick text and ran upstairs to peel herself out of the wet clothes and get into something dry for the short walk into the town centre. She retied her hair into a messy bun and headed back downstairs to raid her mum's cupboard for a waterproof before pulling on her wellies.

"Do you want to come with me?"

Cressida eyed the witch. *If I can lie under the coat.*

Fi sighed, but she nodded and allowed the wyrm to cuddle up inside the jacket. Holding the small animal was like hugging a little hot water bottle.

"We should really get you a carrier," Fi mused out loud. She didn't hear any protests from her familiar, so she pulled out her phone and made a note to look up pet carriers later. She left the house and headed out into the thick rain.

Fi pushed into the café. The doorstep was clear, and Fi guessed Steve had taken the pumpkins inside to protect them from the pelting rain. The bell gave a muffled tinkle as she rushed in – Steve had already taken steps to protect his sensitive hearing. Four heads turned to watch her enter.

Steve looked pointedly at the puddle forming on the floor where she stood. She might as well not have bothered to change her clothes. She stamped her feet and plastered a bright smile on her face.

"Sorry I'm late. What do you think, Effie?"

Effie glided over and kissed her cheek. Fi fought the urge to rub her face. The woman was wearing bright red lipstick and it had probably left a mark. "I think you need to sort your hair out. I've heard of volume, but this is something else."

"I meant, what do you think about the café?"

"It's fabulous. Steve's done a fantastic job and it will be ready for the grand opening."

"Are you sure?" Steve asked, wringing his hands together. "Because I've been working night and day but there's still so much to do. I've got to finish the mural and the stock isn't all out yet and these dust sheets need to go, and I still can't work the stupid machine." He shot a glare at the chrome coffee maker sitting on the side.

"Why don't you give it another go, Fi looks like she needs a hot drink."

"Yes please." Fi smiled encouragingly and Steve walked over to the machine like a man on a mission.

They watched with growing anticipation as he tamped down the Goblin Blend ground beans and fitted the sump to the right slot with no trouble. Then he placed a clean cup under the nozzle and checked the water supply before he pressed a couple of buttons. A promising gurgling noise filled the room, and everyone smiled at the werewolf.

Steve grinned back and gave a thumbs up. Behind him, the machine shuddered. The werewolf turned back to the coffee maker and backed away as it vibrated harder and harder. Then it stopped. Silence filled the room. Fi didn't dare to breathe.

As if it couldn't stand the tension, the machine gave another spurt and the water connection broke loose, spraying clear liquid across the room. Under the coat, Cressida jumped at the sudden noise and Fi winced as the wyrm's sharp claws dug into her skin.

*What's that? Are we under attack?*

Fi patted her familiar and whispered soothing words of comfort about it only being a mean coffee machine. She smiled at herself; she was becoming a proper pet mum.

Effie patted Steve on the shoulder. "Never mind, Fi can fix it."

Fi stopped nodding along. "What?"

"You're good with machines, you can sort it."

Fi gaped at Effie and Steve's twin expressions of complete confidence in her. Yes, she did have a gift with technology, but she worked with computers. She wasn't sure that a coffee maker counted as technology, and her success rate wasn't exactly one hundred percent; things had as much chance of blowing up around her power as they did of getting fixed.

"Sure, I guess I can take a look…"

"Excellent. I knew you could help us," Effie said with a smile.

"Do you mean you've seen that I'll fix it?" Fi couldn't keep the hope out of her voice. Effie's visions were always accurate, if she'd seen that the coffee machine was fixed, then Fi could do it.

"Oh no, but I know you can do it."

Fi's face fell. She wanted to say something, but the door burst open.

# Chapter 10

A middle-aged woman flung herself into the café, panting hard.

"Kathryn, what are you doing here?" Fi's mother took a step forward.

Kathryn's eyes gleamed with excitement. "Have you heard?"

"Heard what?"

"About Sita?"

"What about her?"

"Someone's broken into the florists." Kathryn's voice sang with triumph in her proclamation.

"I'd better go show her some support," Nell said. "Fi, you can come with me."

"What? Why?"

"You're the Magical Liaison Office agent here. Sita is a member of the WWWI; she will need support and you need to check that the authorities are doing a thorough job to solve this heinous crime."

Fi didn't point out that she was meant to be working on a murder case. There was no point arguing with her mother. Instead, she sighed. The promise of a hot coffee had completely disappeared, and she now had to head back into the wet.

"I'm coming too," Effie announced.

Her mother smiled and led the way outside. Kathryn hovered at her shoulder giving more details. Fi stared at the pavement and stepped over a stream of dirty water flowing through the cobbled street. She wrapped her hands around her familiar, pulling some heat from the toasty dragon-like creature. Under her coat, Cressida squirmed.

*Stop it, your hands are freezing.*

"I need your warmth. If you're going to keep wriggling, you can walk."

The wyrm gave a final twist and stayed still, although Fi noticed she had angled her body in such a way that her claws dug into Fi's stomach with each step. Fi looked up as they arrived at the florists. Blue and white police tape criss-crossed over the broken window.

"Who would do such a thing?" her mother asked, poking her head past the tape and peeking inside. "Where's Sita?"

Kathryn jerked her head. "That way." She walked around to the back of the shop with Nell close behind.

Fi traipsed after them both. This was a break in, nothing to do with magic. As they rounded the corner, the group came face to face with a gigantic owlbear. Fi stopped and stared. She had never seen Sita's pet up close before, and she wasn't relishing the opportunity now. She backed away, clutching Cressida closely.

The creature narrowed his golden eyes and let out an ear-piercing shriek. Cressida risked the rain and peeked her head out from Fi's coat.

*Why are we about to fight an owlbear?*

"We're not trying to fight…"

The owlbear rushed at them, clawed arms outstretched and hooked beak open. Fi's mum made a complicated movement with her hands and the beast stopped mid leap. It shrieked again, twisting in anger. The creature managed to move forward an inch against Nell's magic. Ice flowed from Kathryn's wrinkled hand to create a barrier between the witches and the owlbear.

"Help!" her mother shouted, beads of sweat forming on her forehead.

Fi stood there, stunned. Her power couldn't form a barrier, it could only destroy, and she didn't want to hurt Sita's pet.

The owlbear's talons clawed at the ice. It would be on them in seconds. Fi gathered her power to her hands in a ball of electricity. She had no choice. She would protect her mother. She held out her hand and took aim.

Sita appeared behind her pet. "What's going on, Fluff–?"

The wizard ducked as Fi shifted her arm and released her power into the wall behind Sita. The wizard turned slowly and took in the charred brick, still sparking with the remnants of Fi's magic.

The owlbear screamed a third time and attacked the barrier with renewed ferocity.

Sita turned back to the three witches, mouth gaping before she composed herself. "Oh, it's you." She brushed her hands on her apron. "Could you let Fluffy down? You're making him anxious." She took in their faces. "Don't worry. Down, Fluffy, these are our friends."

The beast twisted its head to look at its owner before it sat down and wagged its stubby feathered tail. Even seated, it towered over six feet tall. Sita stroked its back, and it bent its head so the petite wizard could scratch behind its ear tufts. Fi tried to puzzle out where the feathers ended and the fur began, but it was such a natural join of tawny colours that she couldn't make it out.

"Sorry about that, I just didn't feel safe at the shop without Fluffy, so I told him to guard the place. He takes his duties very seriously, don't you Fluffkins?" She did a double take at Fi. "Goodness gracious, Fi, what happened?"

Fi touched her hair self-consciously. "Just the wind."

"Yes, well, now that's out of the way." Nell brushed her hands on her tailored trousers. "Perhaps we can help. How are you?" She walked forward and embraced the younger woman, planting a dry kiss on one cheek.

Sita sighed. "Not good. I just can't understand it."

"Why don't we come in and make a cup of tea?" Nell asked. Fi rolled her eyes. It was typical of her mother to take charge.

The older witch placed an arm around Sita and led her back to the shop. "Didn't you have the wards up?"

Sita shook her head as she bent to pick up a bunch of brightly coloured flowers from the floor. She placed them with care into a metal bucket full of water. "That's what I can't understand; of course I set the wards. I checked them this morning and they were still active. I told the police it must have been someone with strong magic to get past, or maybe it was something I hadn't warded against."

Fi's ears pricked up. "What don't you ward against?"

"Well, the spells take a lot of magic and they're quite complicated, so I don't include every single magical creature, just the more obvious ones. I mean, how many wendigos or yetis do we get in Omensford?"

"I've always thought Jeremy was a bit hairy…"

"Now is not the time for jokes, Kathryn! Why don't you put the kettle on?" Nell interrupted.

"But you ward against humans?" Fi tried to get the questioning back on track.

Sita nodded. "Of course, and witches, warlocks and other wizards, and werewolves and fae…"

"Can you get me a list?" It looked like this robbery did fall under her jurisdiction after all.

The wizard nodded again. Fi thought she looked a bit like one of those nodding dogs. "I'll get you a copy of the spell, if it will help."

"It could do."

*What did they take?*

Cressida pushed her way out of Fi's coat and jumped down to the ground. Fi cursed herself inwardly for not asking the obvious question and repeated it for Sita.

"That's the strange thing. They didn't touch the till or take any of the more expensive flowers…" She caught the frown on Fi's face and gestured to some plants. "These orchids are worth over a hundred pounds, and I've got the largest selection of magical plants in the UK. These Cotswold moonflowers are native only to this area of England, very hard to collect and highly sought after for spells and potions…"

"But the thief didn't take them?" Fi interrupted the lecture on magical flora.

"No, they only took the pumpkins."

Fi looked around the shop as her mother and Kathryn pottered about in the tiny lean-to kitchen at the back. Not a single orange pumpkin.

"I had quite the array of decorative squashes too, in all shapes, sizes and colours. All gone. Just before Halloween. I can't understand it at all, I mean you can get pumpkins anywhere this time of year."

"Yeah, it's weird." Fi agreed. And too close to the disappearance of pumpkins at Harris' farm to be a coincidence.

# Chapter 11

A thought entered Fi's head. "You didn't buy your pumpkins from Harris, did you?"

"No, Harris is great for supersized vegetables or, er, oddly shaped ones, but my customers prefer the smaller pumpkins you can use as centrepieces. I can get you the names of my suppliers if you like?"

"Yes please. I'll just take a look around if that's alright?"

"Of course." Sita reached out and placed a hand on Fi's arm. "Thank you."

"For what?"

"Taking an interest. The police seemed to think it was a routine break in."

"I can't promise I can solve it," Fi said quickly.

"That's alright, it's enough to know you're taking it seriously. I'd better go help Nell and Kathryn before they come to blows over the right way to make tea."

Fi surveyed the shop. It was a mess. Flowers lay trampled on the patterned tiles and smears of mud covered the glass, walls and floor.

Fi snapped some pictures in case Detective Ledd was funny about giving her access to the police report. No one liked to be shown up and it sounded like the police hadn't listened to Sita's concerns. Cressida sniffed her way through the room

"Can you smell anything, Cress?"

The wyrm ignored her.

"Cress?" Fi huffed out a sigh. "Cressida?"

*Yes, were you talking to me?*

"Ha. Ha. What can you smell?"

*Plants.*

"Plants? Can you be any more specific?"

*The plants that are here.* She paused and cocked her head to one side. *And pumpkins; they went out through the window. And mud. It smells the same as the earth at Harris' farm.*

Fi tapped out a note on her phone.

"Any people or magic?"

The wyrm shook her head. *Sita's scent is the strongest, and there's a lot of trails from customers, but nothing stronger than yesterday. Maybe whoever is taking the pumpkins can cover their scent?*

"Maybe." Fi added that to her note.

*Your magic is here, too.*

"From the owlbear fight."

*Maybe...* Cressida didn't sound convinced.

"I'll have to look up some spells in the library, see if there's any that can stop people leaving scents. But first, let's go see if any other pumpkins have been taken in town and I need a coffee."

Fi made her excuses and left the florists via the back door. The owlbear lifted his head and regarded them with large golden eyes. It opened its beak and made a horrible choking sound. Fi gathered power to her hands. Sita rushed out just as it coughed up a matted tangle of fur and small animal bones.

"I didn't–" Fi started.

"It's alright. Fluffy coughs up pellets when he's stressed. Did those nasty witches stress you out, Fluffkins? Who's a good boy?"

*That is nasty.*

Fi backed away, sharing a look of disgust with Cressida. The owlbear made soft clicking noises and stayed where it was, turning its head as they passed so it could watch them leave. Fi didn't shake her power off until it was out of sight.

The rain had stopped, and the changeable weather now shone a shaft of bright autumn sunshine on the small town of Omensford. Fi kept her hood down and her eyes open. No pumpkins anywhere on the high street.

One glance through the café's window told Fi that she shouldn't go in for a caffeine fix. Steve shouted something down the phone about inappropriate tarot cards, talking so loudly that his voice carried through the glass windows into the street. Fi hunched her shoulders and hurried past.

She turned into the small supermarket that serviced the town with its essentials and headed to the back. Cressida followed close to her heels, avoiding the attempts to pet her golden scales by weaving between Fi's legs. Fi swore and flung her arms out, seeking support as the wyrm tripped her up. She clutched at a display and realised too late that it was a pyramid of tins. The structure gave way and she fell with it in a crash and thunk of metal. The witch glared at Cressida from her spot on the floor, surrounded by tins. The wyrm hissed.

"Are you laughing? Because if you're laughing…"

*I'm not. I'm not.*

Slightly mollified, Fi heaved herself upright and gave an apologetic wave to the shop owner; Sita's father. Mr Kumar huffed out a sigh and hurried over.

"I hope you are not hurt? Did you bump your head?" His eyes roamed over her voluminous hairdo.

Fi tried in vain to flatten her white hair down. "No, sorry, it was my fault. I'll stack it up."

"Good, see that you do. I have customers to serve." He bustled back to the queue of two people in the shop.

Fi began to restack the tins.

"It was a pyramid." Mr Kumar called from behind the checkout.

Fi started again. Once she had finished to the owner's standards, she headed to the back of the store and used the self-serve machine to make a coffee. Her stomach growled and she bought a chocolate bar to stave off her growing hunger.

"One coffee, one chocolate bar. That will be five pound twenty please, Miss Fi."

She paid with her card and looked around the shop. "No pumpkins in?"

Mr Kumar sighed, "No, it is most unfortunate. Harris supplies my pumpkins, he always has the best shapes, but he told me that his field was ransacked, so I have no supplier this year."

"Can't you use someone else?"

"Oh Miss Fi, if only it were that simple. Orders for the Halloween season are placed far in advance. There are none spare for me, but I have returned to tradition. See?" He held up a turnip. Fi blinked at him, not understanding. "I looked it up. The first jack-o-lanterns were not pumpkins but the humble turnip."

"Are they selling?"

"Not as well as I'd hoped," he admitted. "Do you want one?"

"Er, no thanks, I'm a bit old to carve faces in vegetables." Fi said goodbye and left him to try to offload his turnips on the next customer.

She paused by the door to let in a crying child and his parent.

"We'll just get another pumpkin from the shop, you'll see."

"Did something happen to your pumpkin?" Fi asked. The child peered up at her through tear-filled eyes. He opened his eyes wider and started bawling. Fi pulled her hood up to cover her hideous hair and tried again. "Do you want to stroke my wyrm, she loves children."

*I do not.*

"Come on Cressida, it's for the case." Fi bent down and whispered in her familiar's ear. The wyrm humphed but allowed the boy to stroke her.

"So, what happened?" Fi asked the mum.

"Bloody teenagers is what. We spent ages carving that pumpkin. Little Roy's been so excited to do it, but we put it out last night and this morning; gone. And they messed up the garden too, like they were driving on the lawn, but we never heard a thing. I tell you, there's no respect for people's property nowadays and now I've got to buy another one."

"Did you report it?"

The woman barked out a laugh. "Report it?! It's a bloody pumpkin, what are the police going to do? Come on Roy, let's go ask the nice man if he's got any pumpkins left."

Fi sipped her drink and made a face. Supermarket coffee, urgh. As she left, she heard Mr Kumar trying to convince the mother to get a turnip. "Alas, I have no pumpkins at all, and where will you get one this close to Halloween? But look, see. This is the glorious vegetable that the very first faces were carved in, and for you, I will do two for one."

# Chapter 12

Fi paused on the walk back to her mum's Bed & Breakfast, pulling her hood down and unzipping her coat in the glare of the sun. A crowd of tourists milled around the town hall. It was normal to get more visitors to the town at this time of year; everyone went crazy for supernaturals at Halloween and, being a protected magical area, Omensford had more than its fair share of snap happy tourists. But something about this group made Fi stop. She dumped the disgusting coffee into a bin and pushed her way to the front.

When she reached the police tape, she stopped. The huge Halloween display had been trashed. A young police officer stood just behind the tape, keeping a straight face as the tourists aimed their cameras at him.

"What happened?" Fi asked.

"Sorry, Miss, please stand back. I think there's a bench in the park where you can rest for a bit, but you can't be here today."

"I'm not homeless!" Fi showed him her badge, pleased she still had it on her after this morning's morgue excursion.

The officer stared at her then squinted. "Are you sure that's you?"

"It's me!"

"Only your hair…"

She scowled at him. "Are you going to tell me what happened or am I going to have to call your superior?"

"Alright, well it looks like some vandals destroyed the display."

"I can see that."

"Er…well that's it."

She stared at him. His brown eyes darted around looking for an escape. She felt her power crackle under her skin and her hair began to frizz up even more from the electricity building inside her. The witch fought to control her magic as her stomach growled. The officer swallowed.

"I mean, I'm just here to guard it, make sure no one takes anything. The footage has been sent to the station and they're analysing it now."

Fi followed the guard's gaze to the security camera mounted high on the town hall, its black lens an odd addition to the traditional Cotswold stone building.

"Bit late to worry about protecting the display now it's destroyed. What about the other thefts?"

"You mean the florists? Yes, we've got all the footage we can, and we've asked for witnesses to come forward, but this is a quiet town, everyone in bed by ten. No leads yet."

Fi raised her eyebrows at the policeman. This was a magical town and there were a lot of supernaturals who were out and about during the night, but they might not want to talk to the police. "I want to see that footage."

"Yes, Miss."

Fi turned to go, then spun on her heels. "What's your name?" She jotted it down on her phone, then swore as a camera flash blinded her. Without thinking, she released a small bolt of power, and the tourist dropped a camera to the floor, shaking his hand at the sudden electric shock.

The people immediately around him all looked down at the camera, then to the man, then to Fi and back to the man. They all cheered, took out their own devices and snapped a picture of the real live witch.

Fi turned away and covered her face with her hand, but they kept going. She spotted a dart of gold scurry through the crowd and the flashes stopped as cries of pain and surprise sounded. One woman tripped over her own feet and toppled into another man, setting off a domino effect in the crowd.

Fi fought the urge to film their plight on her phone. It would be so easy; she still had her smartphone in her hand. She glanced down and swore. Her magic had shorted out her own device as well as the man's camera. She covered her hair with the hood again and hurried home as the tourists tried to recover. She needed some food. It was always harder to control her power when she was gripped by strong emotions and the hunger pangs were not helping moderate her mood.

Cressida caught up with her and trotted at her feet.

"Thank you."

*You're welcome. What are familiars for if we can't help you out of a tight spot?*

"You didn't hurt anyone, did you?"

*Just a small nip here and there. I didn't break any skin.*

With a small smile, Fi crouched down and allowed the wyrm to climb up to her favourite spot; curled around the witch's neck.

"Come on, I need to pick up a new phone on the way home."

Chapter 13

Back at the house, Fi made herself a quick sandwich and topped up Cressida's charcoal in her food bowl before sitting down at her computer station. She took a sip of her diet cola and powered on the computer.

Sat in front of the screen, all her concerns in the real world melted away. She forgot her damp clothes and her crazy hair. Instead, she immersed herself in a reality she could understand. Fi synched up her new phone to her cloud account. She held her breath and crossed her fingers as it loaded; she didn't always check her back up timings and she had a lot of important pictures on there.

She let out a sigh of relief as the photos from Harris' farm appeared and scrolled forward. Fi swore. It looked like the pictures from Sita's shop hadn't uploaded. Her fingers drummed the desk as she thought.

Less than a minute later, she scrolled through Sita's social media feeds and found what she was after. Thank you, Sita, for posting every aspect of your life online, she thought as she downloaded photos of the break-in site.

On a whim, she looked up the cost of the orchids Sita had pointed out. Fi let out a soft whistle. The wizard hadn't lied; those things were worth hundreds of pounds. So why hadn't they been taken?

She saved everything to a new virtual case board on her machine. Fi had created the programme to help her order her thoughts, and because she liked the way it reminded her of the cork murder boards on TV detective programmes. She had yet to integrate it with the Magical Liaison Office official software, but she was confident in her own security programmes and now had several boards on her own PC from previous crimes she'd helped to solve.

This one though…Fi searched online for anything on the murder or the break in. The local paper – the Omensford Gazette – had separate articles up for both. And the shop break-in was linked to the vandalism in town. Fi winced at the headline; *Smashing Pumpkins - Concerns Grow as Vandals Raid Local Florist.* At least the murder was covered more tastefully; *Man Found Dead in Field.*

Fi guessed the police hadn't released any information about the body missing its head, or the editor might have been tempted to make some headless horseman puns.

She linked the articles into her corkboard and stared at the screen. It was all connected. It had to be; a murder in a pumpkin field and all the pumpkins in town going missing. It was too big a coincidence to be a coincidence. She wrote the word 'pumpkin' in large letters in the centre, followed by five question marks.

A quick internet search for creatures that might be interested in pumpkins surfaced several videos of dogs eating the innards and a fat hedgehog trying to get inside a large pumpkin. Cute, but nothing that could devour an entire field of the orange vegetables.

Fi broadened the search and got a list of Halloween films that related to pumpkins. She skipped past cartoon drawings of Charlie Brown and pursed her lips as she thought. Maybe the list of creatures not covered by Sita's ward would give her something to go on.

She broadened her search again to cover unnatural goings on in the Cotswolds. There were the usual reports of supernatural sightings and one blurry photo of a giant 'beast' roaming the fields. Fi shook her head; it was probably someone's cat taking a dump on the edge of a field.

The bedroom door opened by itself and her familiar ambled in.

*I thought you were getting showered.* Cressida hopped up onto the bed and curled up in the centre of Fi's video game themed bedspread.

"In a minute, I'm on the verge of a breakthrough…"

*And here I thought you were on the verge of a date.*

"What? That's not 'til…" Fi glanced at the clock in the corner of her screen and swore. Mort was due to pick her up in twenty minutes.

*We need to talk about your language.*

"Not now! I've got to shower!" Fi barged out of her room and ran to the family bathroom. She hopped from one foot to the other as she waited for the shower to heat up. "Come on, come on, any time you like."

She didn't think the sentient house was spiteful, but it seemed to take forever for the water to run hot.

As soon as it was warm enough that she wouldn't wince getting in, she stripped off and stepped into the shower. The water immediately heated up to scalding temperature. Fi emitted a small shriek and adjusted the taps.

She glared up at the ceiling. "Really?" she asked the house.

No reply.

She shook her head and went back to getting washed. She lathered her hair with shampoo and tried to get a brush through it while shaving her legs all at the same time.

Fi wasn't even surprised when she slipped and landed hard against the glass in the walk-in shower. She swore and gave up on her hair, focusing her attention on the rest of her body. In five minutes flat, she was out of the shower and wrapped in a towel.

Fi ran across the hall to her bedroom, almost colliding with a shocked Effie and Cirian on the landing. She waved an apology and slammed her door shut behind her. Fi was in such a rush, she didn't even have time to feel embarrassed at guests seeing her practically naked.

She searched through her cupboard for clean clothes. Cressida watched on with interest.

*I told you that you should have done some washing.*

Clearly their time working together was over. Fi chucked a t-shirt at the wyrm and carried on digging. She found a skater style dress and a clean pair of leggings and tugged them on over her slightly damp skin. The leggings stuck part way up her thighs and Fi started a series of wild acrobatic exercises to finish getting them on.

She took her small make-up bag downstairs to finish getting ready in front of the big mirror in the hallway – it always had the best lighting.

Her mum crossed her path going downstairs. She paused and looked her daughter up and down. "Is that how you're going out?"

"It's a haunted house, it'll be dark."

Nell arched an eyebrow and pursed her lips, but mercifully stayed silent.

"Oh, let her be, Nell. She needs to feel comfortable if she's going to seduce the handsome doctor." Effie joined them on the stairs.

Fi's cheeks heated. "It's a date, that's all." She was not comfortable talking about any sort of seduction in front of her mother.

"We were all young once." Effie shot a wink at Fi. "But I'd do something about your hair if I were you…"

Fi's hand strayed up to her head. She moaned and tugged, then swore. The hairbrush was stuck in there.

"I can lend you some conditioner, if you like?" Cirian's musical voice floated across the room.

Fi blinked up at him and nodded weakly.

# Chapter 14

The elven conditioner must have been made of miracles, Fi thought, as she ran her fingers through her tamed mane for the seventeenth time. No wonder elves always looked perfect. Not only did they have glamour, they also had styling products that actually worked. Some people had all the luck.

Fi applied another coat of lip gloss to her mouth.

*You're going to frighten him away if you look like a trout.*

The witch glared at her familiar. "I don't look like a fish. Don't you have a stove to curl up in front of?"

*Gladly. As soon as you've left. Your feelings are making me anxious.*

"What feelings?" Fi pushed away the butterflies flying around in her stomach and smoothed down her hair again.

*Don't you know anything about familiars?*

"I think it's clear that I don't. Here, I thought they were meant to help the person they were paired with."

The small wyrm snorted, but a knock on the door interrupted whatever pearls of wisdom she'd been about to disclose on witch-familiar bonds.

Fi opened the back door, glad that the house didn't act up as she greeted Mort.

"Hi."

"Hi yourself." He bent forward to kiss her, but she turned her head so his lips pressed against her cheek, her face heating at the display of affection in front of her mother and judgmental familiar.

Nell put down her crochet and stood to greet Mort. "Dr De'ath, won't you come in for a cup of coffee before you go?"

"Now Nell, let the lovebirds go out." Effie tugged on Nell's silk shirtsleeve.

"Yeah, Mum, sorry but we've got to get going or we'll be late." Fi practically shoved Mort out of the door.

*Yes, go.* Cressida agreed as she settled on her cushion in front of the aga. She flicked her tongue at Fi as if to emphasise her point.

"I wouldn't have minded going in for coffee, I like your mum."

The same way a puppy liked playing with a snake, Fi thought. "I prefer being alone, with you."

Mort reached up and tucked a strand of silky hair behind her ear. He bent down and whispered, "So do I." His hot breath brushed against her skin and Fi shuddered.

She turned towards him, and he captured her lips in a thorough kiss. The house slammed its shutters twice and Mort pulled away. Fi's head span when he broke the kiss.

He frowned up at the house. "I don't think your mum likes me."

"Mum? Oh, no, it's just the house. It's sort of alive or conscious or something. It gets protective and can be judgmental. Sorry."

"Don't be sorry. I'm glad you've got people, and houses, who look after you." He checked his watch. "We'd better go. Wouldn't want to be late."

## Chapter 15

Mort parked his expensive four by four in the field next to a souped-up Volkswagen Polo with flashy gold wheel rims and a spoiler almost the same size as the car. Fi avoided looking directly at the neon paintwork under the temporary spotlights in case she went blind.

She picked her way across the mud, wishing that she'd worn her wellies instead of her converse trainers. She'd thought that her shoes would be safe, after all the definition of a haunted house was that it was inside; the clue's in the name. Her mistake was forgetting that, in order to reach the converted barn, they had to traverse a field.

They passed a couple of lacklustre protestors waving signs and chanting that magic was evil and supernaturals were the cause of all the world's problems. Fi ignored them as they passed. Crazy anti-magic protestors.

Mort paused at the temporary cashier's desk and handed over a note to the bored-looking lady seated on a folding chair.

She wore a pair of fluffy black cat ears stuck to a headband and pointed to the path.

"That way for a spectacularly spooky time. Watch out for things that go bump in the night. This activity is not for pregnant women, people with heart conditions or those with a nervous disposition." She handed them a form. "Sign here to say you accept the risks."

Fi took out her new phone and shone the torch over the piece of paper. "It says here that you're not responsible for injury or theft on the premises."

The woman shrugged and pulled her scarf around her neck more tightly. "If you want to enter, you sign. If not…" She shrugged again under her thick coat.

"If you don't want to, we can go somewhere else." There was Mort again, giving her an out, being a considerate gentleman. He was too good for her.

Fi frowned, more at the thought of Mort being too good for her than at the form, accepted the chewed biro and signed.

Mort grinned down at her, signed his name, and they began the walk down the dirt path to the barn. A young couple bumped her as they passed, arms linked together and giggling, anxious to go in and get their scare on. Fi shivered in the cold night air and Mort shrugged off his soft, lambswool coat and draped it over her shoulders.

She smiled up at him. Her gaze fell on the couple in front, and she linked her arm through Mort's, copying them. Fi could hear the smile on Mort's face as he patted her hand and drew her closer.

"Not scared, are you?"

"Terrified." Fi let her voice go all breathy in the world's worst Marilyn Monroe impression and Mort let out a throaty chuckle.

"Don't be, I'm the most frightening thing here." He was being playful, but there was something in his voice that rang true; an edge of pain or regret under the banter.

Fi looked up at him, about to reply when a zombie shuffled out in front of them and groaned. Fi shrieked. Mort pulled her closer. Fi's power flooded her veins, and she gathered it to her free hand, ready to blast the undead creature back to the afterlife.

"Cool trick!" said the zombie, its yellow eyes staring at her right hand where a ball of electrical power glowed. Mort took out his keyring and shone a pocket torch at the zombie. Under the bright light, the greenish makeup and stick-on scars were more obvious.

Fi shook off her power and a few stray sparks fell to the ground. "Cool costume," she replied with a smile.

Of course, there would be actors here, or, she squinted at the zombie, teenagers looking for some quick cash with their friends. She shuddered again.

She had come this close to blasting an innocent human. She took a deep breath, wishing that her magic could do something more useful than hurt people. Fi crossed her arms and hugged herself. She couldn't use her power on humans. She wouldn't. She had to keep it under control.

"Really nice stitching," Mort leaned in closer and admired a fake sutured wound on the actor's forehead.

The zombie grinned, revealing white teeth. "Thanks. Anyway, got to get back to it. Enjoy the scares." He schooled his face back into a slack jawed expression and walked stiffly towards the next group of people.

Fi and Mort carried on, both silent. Fi rolled her eyes as they passed a fake gravestone.

"Noah Scape? Really?"

Mort laughed again. Fi was tempted to read out all the punny names if she got to hear that laugh each time, so rich, with a touch of something deeper and full of promise behind the joy. But then a vampire leapt out from behind the gravestone of Dr. Acula.

He leered at them with red eyes and sharp teeth. Fi narrowed her eyes at the faint glow around his pupils. Were those contacts or was the haunted house employing real vampires?

"Velcome to the Cotsvolds Haunted House," he said in his best fake Transylvanian accent. "Bevare, for those who go in do not always come out!" The actor let out a loud laugh then disappeared in a cloud of smoke.

The effect was slightly ruined by the corner of his cape catching on the tombstone and a muffled swearword in a more British accent floating through the dissipating mist.

Mort laughed and Fi joined in. This was fun, Fi thought as they strolled down the path to the barn. Outside of the month of October, the barn was a utilitarian storage unit for hay and tractors, but the owners had seen the potential in the huge space and had transformed it into an impressive display, worthy of a Hollywood set.

Somehow, the barn had been reshaped to resemble a gothic house, complete with fake iron railings and stone effect gargoyles. Fake windows were backlit, and shadows flitted across the panes. An actor dressed as a mad scientist took their tickets and opened the door. She bowed them through with a hammy evil laugh.

"Do make sure you don't disturb the experiments," she wheezed before allowing the door to swing shut behind them.

# Chapter 16

Fi took in the gloomy entryway. Three closed doors stared back at her. She looked up at Mort. The flickering light did strange things to the shadows on his face. For a second, her heart pumped against her chest, and she forgot how to talk.

"Make your choice!" A voice boomed out of the darkness. Fi spun around, until she spotted the speaker high up in a corner, only half hidden behind a spider's web.

"Which way shall we go?" she asked.

"Lady's choice." He gave a half bow.

Fi playfully swatted him on the arm, ignoring her chest where her heart was now turning somersaults for reasons that had nothing to do with fear. She regarded the doors again. One had a huge spiderweb over it. Nope. Not that one. She knew better than to choose the one that was completely blank; things that appeared normal often covered up the very worst experiences. Instead, she selected the door that had a large eye rotating in its brass socket. It literally stared back at her as she pushed it open.

The room was dark, so Mort and Fi shuffled in.

"Don't let go of my hand," Fi said.

"Don't worry, I won't," Mort replied with feeling as he squeezed her palm. Fi's stomach joined in the internal gymnastics.

The door creaked shut and dim lights flicked on, reflected back out of dirty mirrors. A mirror maze!

"This should be easy!" Fi exclaimed with a grin. She strode forward, confident she had it figured out. All they had to do was not walk into their own reflections. Simple. She turned a corner and slammed straight into a mirror.

"Ouch!" She rubbed her nose, blinking back the tears forming in her eyes.

"That looked like it hurt, let me see." Mort took her cheeks in his hands and gently probed her nose with his thumbs.

"I'm fine, really." Fi tried to brush him off, but then his chocolate brown eyes captured hers. She could feel his breath whisper over her face. Suddenly, Fi felt hot. Why was the temperature up so high in the barn? Mort leaned in.

A wail echoed through the maze. He sighed and planted a kiss on her forehead. "Come on, I think that means we're taking too long."

He stepped away and took Fi's hand again. She pushed down her regret at the missed kiss and followed him this time, keeping her free hand trailing against the mirrors so she didn't bash into another one. Mort disappeared through a gap in the wall and Fi's heart raced until she realised he'd found the way out. He tugged her hand and she followed through into a playroom.

An empty rocking chair squeaked back and forth, making long shadows in the thread of white moonlight that pooled into the middle of the poorly lit room. Fi's power hummed under her skin. She closed her eyes for a second and focused; able to feel the devices used to make the spooky effects. Fi opened her eyes. She'd thought that knowing how the illusion worked would make it less scary. It didn't.

They both jumped as girlish laughter rang through the room followed by a thud as a small rubber ball dropped from a shelf and rolled across the wooden floor towards them. Fi stepped over the ball and looked over her shoulder, curious to see where it would stop.

She screamed, unprepared for the small girl in a white lacy nightdress standing directly behind them. Fi stepped backwards, almost falling in her shock. Mort held her steady, a solid, warm presence at her side.

The girl bent down and picked up the ball before skipping over to a corner, singing an offkey lullaby. She turned the handle on a giant box decorated with creepy clowns near the exit and a slow tune filled the room.

Fi tensed. Nothing happened. They waited. Nothing. The girl skipped across to the window that was actually a screen and stared at them through her long greasy hair as she pushed a rocking horse in time with the chair. So, they had to move before anything would happen.

Fi took a deep breath and told her heart to slow down as they crept across the room. It didn't help.

She still jumped when the actor leapt out of the box like a giant jack-in-the-box, complete with clown make-up and helium balloons. Mort squeezed her hand with a jolt of fear and they both backed into the wall before running into the next room, followed by the sound of the clown's laugh.

"Close the door!" screamed the girl behind them. Fi slammed it and sank back against the cool wood. Her heart hammered against her rib cage.

They were in a small corridor between rooms. Ahead of them, they heard a scream followed by a nervous giggle. Another couple.

"I don't know if I can take much more of this," Mort spoke softly. Fi patted his hand. He was shaking.

"What happened to my big, strong protector?" she teased as her breathing returned to normal.

"Demons from the underworld are one thing, but ghost girls give me the creeps."

Fi stood on her tiptoes and kissed his cheek. "Don't worry, I'll protect you." She smiled, as if the words made her braver and gathered her power to her hand. She was a powerful witch and a few special effects in a haunted house wouldn't scare her. "You know she was just an actor, right?"

"Come on, let's go through to the next room."

# Chapter 17

Fi nodded and led the way. The door opposite them was covered with fake spider webs. Not a good sign. She opened it and walked through, straight into sticky webbing. She thrashed around, trying to get it off, but the webbing became more tangled the more she struggled. Fi huffed out a sigh and kept moving forward, one arm in front of her face so the sticky stuff didn't get in her eyes, and the other hand pulling Mort along behind her as she climbed the stairs.

Halfway up the staircase, a huge spider dropped from the ceiling straight in front of them. Fi reacted on instinct and shot out a blast of power into its fat body. The arachnid exploded in a spray of plastic and rubber. The smell of burning tyres filled the room. Fi coughed, choking on the fumes. More spiders dropped from the room, dangling on thick threads. Fake spiders. Fi's brain caught up with her eyes. Oops. She forced her power back down and took a step forward.

The fire alarm blared through the house. Fi looked around guiltily. Had she done that? Pale green lights came on, illuminating fire exit routes and the remaining spiders with an otherworldly glow.

The door behind them opened and the tall nightmare clown burst through the spiders. "Everyone out, this is not a drill. Follow me to the nearest exit." He pushed past them and led the way upstairs, brushing past the dancing spiders and sending them spinning.

Mort groaned behind her and stepped up close. Fi looked over her shoulder and saw the ghost girl behind them. Fi stifled her smile and moved to one side to let Mort go ahead. He gave her a tight smile and walked in front.

"Shouldn't we be going downstairs to get out?" he asked the clown.

The actor's bright red wig bobbed as he shook his head. "The fastest way is through here."

It occurred to Fi that if this were a horror film, maybe they shouldn't follow a creepy clown or trust a demon child to get them out. What if they were really serial killers and this was a trap?

Her mind started to go down a dark path. She'd watched enough scary movies as a teenager. There were so many ways to be murdered…well she wasn't going down without a fight. Her magic bubbled under her skin, and she kept it there, ready to use.

The clown ignored the painted arrows directing people left and turned right at the top of the staircase and opened another door. They followed him into a murder room. Rusty metal weapons glinted in the ghoulish green light as they swung on racks suspended from the ceiling. A body lay to one side and a large dark stain spread out from it, staining the white tiles.

"Shouldn't we help him?" Fi asked as the clown stepped over the corpse, heading for the door.

The clown shot her a look. "It's a mannequin." To prove his point, he kicked the body with one oversized shoe, and it flipped over, revealing a blank face.

"Oh, right, of course," Fi mumbled.

The clown selected another door with a large glowing green exit sign over it. There was nothing there.

"Well, go on." The clown was annoyed.

Mort let go of Fi's hand, stepped forward and disappeared.

"What the–?" Fi started. Then she saw. It was a slide. Of course. She sat down and pushed off into the almost sheer drop. Her dress bunched up around her bottom as she slid down the twisty slide. It dumped her onto a foam mat coated with rubber and she scrambled to get out of the way as the clown followed after her. She slipped twice, building a sweat as she struggled to find a way off the spongy crash mat.

Mort helped her up and she sank against him, panting after her fight with the mat. The ghost girl came down last, her dark hair flying behind her as she exited the slide. She gave up on standing and crawled to the end of the mat, looking more like something from a horror film. Mort turned away and Fi noticed he put her between his body and the actor. So much for chivalry.

"What now?" Fi asked the clown.

He fished in his costume and pulled out a walkie talkie, before stepping away to talk to whoever was on the other end.

"We cleared the playroom, stairs, and the murderer's hideout. Over." The clown disappeared around the side of the house and Fi couldn't hear what he said next.

Slow minutes passed and Fi's adrenaline cut out, leaving her cold and tired as they waited outside the house for the clown to return.

"OK, it's all clear. Looks like one of the spiders blew up in the spider room." Fi opened her mouth then closed it again as the clown barrelled on. "They've blocked that route off to be sure, but you can go back in if you like."

Fi shook her head then looked up at Mort.

"Suit yourself," said the clown. "If you speak to the lady on the tickets, she can give you a new timeslot for another night. We're open until the fifth of November so plenty of time to come back. Here's two tickets for a complimentary cup of mulled apple juice at the cider stand. Come on Claire, we'd better go back in and set up, they're opening the doors in ten minutes."

The clown and the ghost headed back into the house via a side door and Mort sighed.

"Sorry, this wasn't exactly the end to our date I had in mind."

Fi smiled and snatched the drinks tickets from his hand. "Who says the date is over?"

# Chapter 18

Mort rewarded her with a grin that dimpled one cheek. He was annoyingly handsome sometimes, Fi thought, as they walked to the cider stand. She handed over their tickets and took her cup of mulled apple juice, enjoying the warmth that spread through her hands as she held the plastic cup.

The rich scent of cinnamon and other autumn spices floated in the cold night air and Fi inhaled, instantly transported back to her childhood when her mother had brewed mulled juices and ciders in her large cauldron, often accompanied by baking. Fi opened her eyes. She could murder a warm apple scone about now.

"Penny for your thoughts."

"Hmmm?"

"You looked so happy, content. What were you thinking about?"

"Just a happy memory." Fi's eyes lit on the menu next to the stand. They sold hotdogs and, yes, not quite a scone, but close enough. "A piece of apple cake please."

"Make that two." Mort paid and the bored looking man behind the stand handed over two huge slices of cake. The doctor tried to juggle everything until Fi stepped in and took his drink from him. They looked around for somewhere to sit.

Fi spotted a bench. "Over there."

They walked past the maze made from stacked haybales. Screams sounded from behind the walls as thrill-seekers braved the horrors of Freddy's Nightmare Maze. Fi kept walking past a wooden sign for a Pumpkin Patch, underneath the printed letters was a scrawl, warning visitors to 'watch out for the pumpkin king'. Fi hoped no one was waiting to jump out at them while they enjoyed their snacks. The scent of sweet, cooked apple mixed with cinnamon and ginger was driving her taste buds wild and she could feel the saliva building in her mouth in anticipation.

A strange sucking sound came from the treeline, and she stopped walking, aware that Mort had halted.

"Something's wrong," he said, looking pale in the thin moonlight.

Fi looked around. It was a pretty poor effort at a pumpkin patch; there were only some scraggly vines and leaves trailing through mud. No orange vegetables in sight. The hairs on the back of Fi's neck lifted. She looked longingly at the bench and sighed. So close.

Instead, she took a step towards the fence, intending to set the drinks down so she could get her phone out when she tripped. Mulled apple juice went flying and Fi swore as she landed on something sticky lying in the mud.

Mort was by her side in an instant, kneeling next to her without a care for the dirt staining his dark jeans. She pushed herself to her knees and fumbled for her phone. She got the torch on and stared as its beam illuminated a body.

Fi didn't need Mort's medical degree to know that she was kneeling next to a corpse.

It was missing a head.

# Chapter 19

"Why is it that every time there's a decapitated body, you're at the crime scene?" Detective Ledd asked, notebook in hand.

"It's not like I want to find bodies!" Fi kicked at the ground. She knew they should have stayed in playing videogames, at least the corpses on screen were fake.

The detective made a noise like he didn't believe her.

"You're not seriously considering me as a suspect?"

He raised one bushy eyebrow, an expression that made him look like a fish suffering from stomach troubles, then his face relaxed into its usual jowly lines. "No," the detective sighed, "you have got an alibi for the whole evening and video footage confirming you were in the house at the time."

"Great." There was that eyebrow raise again. "I mean, not great, obviously, but you'll let me sit in on the interviews."

He looked her up and down. Fi pulled Mort's coat tighter over her blood-stained clothes. She stared him down.

"Fine." Detective Ledd stalked away to terrorise a young officer who looked about twelve into rounding up everyone who was here this evening.

Mort strode over and offered Fi a piece of cake. She stared at it.

"It's fresh. You should eat, the sugar will help with the shock..."

Fi blinked up at him through a mouthful of cake. She didn't need reassurance that the apple deliciousness would help her; sugar and caffeine were her go to answers for all of life's problems. It was a shame the cider stall didn't serve coffee, or she'd be set.

"Thanks," she said around the crumbs. "Any idea on time of death?"

He shook his head. "That's for the coroner to say, but they were dead when we arrived in the field."

"How do you know?" The memory of him stopping and saying something was wrong surfaced in Fi's mind. How did his powers work anyway?

She knew he had a link to the God of Death, but did that mean he could sense corpses? Her mind wandered as she imagined what it would be like to sense bodies. What if he walked through a graveyard?

"We would have seen or heard something if it happened after we arrived."

"Oh yeah, right. Of course."

"And...I could sense it."

"How?" It wasn't exactly a subtle question, but it was the best Fi could manage in between bites.

"I just…know. I can sense death, especially when it's so recent. It's like the soul calls to me, and I want to help, but I can't guide them to the underworld, it's not part of my power."

"What exactly is your power?"

"I don't know how to explain…"

Fi turned away and stared across the field where the scene of crime forensic team were already at work around the body. He didn't know how to explain, or he didn't want to let her in? And after he already knew everything about her destructive powers.

"…but maybe I can show you sometime."

Fi looked back at him and cocked her head to one side. "Alright. It's a date."

"You still want to go out again? Even after this?" He stepped forward.

Fi swallowed hard. "At least it's not boring, but maybe next time I should pick the activity."

His lips curved upwards, and one hand moved to stroke her silky white hair.

"Are you coming then?" Detective Ledd's jarring voice ruined the moment.

"Go on," Mort whispered. "I'll wait for you."

Fi couldn't help the slow smile that crept over her face. She stuffed the final bite of apple cake into her mouth and caught up with the detective as he headed for the house. The cake was almost too good, with the perfect amount of crunchy brown sugar caramelised on top. She had to get the recipe.

# Chapter 20

One by one, the visitors came into the office that Detective Ledd had commandeered for the interviews. It was a small room, containing an oversized desk that dominated the space. The detective sat in the wheeled office chair while Fi rearranged herself in the folding chair someone had found for her. A matching chair sat opposite the desk.

For each paying guest, the detective noted their name, number and address in his book and asked the same questions.

"Where were you this evening?"

And they'd answer, "In the house." Or "In the maze". Sometimes they'd describe the route they took. Fi's ears perked up as they named rooms she hadn't even seen in the haunted house.

"Did you notice anything suspicious?"

And the inevitable answer, "In a haunted house? No. Nothing seemed out of the ordinary."

And the detective would tell them that he'd be in touch if he needed anything else. Fi yawned. Then an officer ushered in a man gripping a cardboard sign like it was a shield. He glared over at them.

"It's my right to protest. You can't stop me."

Detective Ledd looked up from his leatherbound notebook. "We shall see. Now Mr…"

"O'Riley. Finn O'Riley."

"Where were you this evening?"

The man leaned back on his chair and balanced his foot on the opposite knee. He made a loud sucking sound as he considered the question. "Out front with Delores all night. That lady on the front desk will tell you. The one dressed like a cat. It's not right. They glamourise all this supernatural shi…I mean, stuff and it's not normal."

Fi kept her face neutral. She worked for the Magical Liaison Office, and she was a witch; prejudices were nothing new to her. But she couldn't help saying something. "You do know that some supernatural races have been on this planet for longer than humans, Mr O'Riley?"

He sneered at her and rubbed his nose with gloved hands. "So, they say. How do we know, hey?"

"There's masses of archaeological evidence as well as…"

"Thank you, Ms Blair." The detective held up a hand. "So, you don't like supernaturals or people who 'glamourise' them. I suppose this haunted house falls into that category?"

O'Riley grunted.

"And how much do you hate them?"

O'Riley's eyes narrowed. "The world would be a better place if they weren't here. Us humans should be joining together against them, not dressing up and pretending to be them."

"So, you don't like humans who dress up as supernaturals either…" Another grunt. "Enough to kill someone?"

"What?" O'Riley stopped nodding along so quickly, he could have got whiplash. "No. I protest, sure, but I don't kill people. Is that what this is about? Was it one of the freaks? The police out there didn't tell us anything. Can you even kill supernaturals? I mean, they're already undead or something, right?"

Fi's mouth dropped open at his ignorance, but the detective spoke first.

"We'll be in touch Mr O'Riley."

Fi fidgeted in her seat as the detective nodded to the door, dismissing the protestor.

"What was that?"

"What?"

"You let him go!"

"I didn't have any evidence to charge him with. That's what we look for. Evidence."

"But he hates supernaturals and humans who like them."

"That's not a crime, Ms Blair. And besides, he's human, how could he rip someone's head off?"

Fi shuffled on her chair. He had a point. She hadn't sensed any magic from him but… "He might not be human."

Detective Ledd sighed. "We've got his details. Now, are you going to keep badgering me about this or can we finish up with the witnesses because we've still got to interview the staff."

He yawned.

"You look tired. Late night gaming?" Fi could sympathise.

He pursed his lips. "Just talking to someone."

Fi raised an eyebrow. "Someone?"

"No one. Can we get on with this now?"

Fi nodded, forcing down her curiosity over his private life as the detective called in the staff members. The only ones not in the house were the victim – provisionally identified as Trevor Knight, an actor who was meant to portray the fearsome pumpkin king – and the actor playing Freddy Krueger in the nightmare maze.

Detective Ledd rubbed his eyes. "Well, they've all got alibis for the night, and we'll confirm what we can with the camera footage. I'll make sure you get a copy. Just the manager to go."

A large man stepped into the tiny room, his presence drawing the light and making the space seem even more cramped. The electric light gleamed off his bald head, creating a strange halo effect. Fi wondered if he polished his head. It was so shiny that she couldn't keep her eyes off it as he sat down on the seat. Bulkier than the detective, he carried himself with the air of someone who knows what every muscle in his body is called and the small chair creaked under his stocky form.

"Mr Denzel?"

The man nodded in agreement and held out a thick hand. He shook the detective's and Larry winced in the firm grip. Fi sat on her own hands and gave him a small smile. He didn't seem bothered at all that she didn't shake his hand. "At your service. I don't normally work the weekend shift, but soon as I heard, I came down."

"You own this establishment?"

He puffed out his chest and beamed at the two of them behind the desk. "Five years running! Halloween and Christmas events. Next year, I'm doing an Easter scene too; egg hunts, bunnies. The lot."

"You don't seem very concerned…"

"Well, it's tragic isn't it, but life goes on as they say and it's always a risk that actors are a bit unreliable…"

"You do know he's dead?" Fi couldn't help herself from interrupting.

"Yes," the man's brow furrowed, "tragic, as I said."

Fi narrowed her eyes and tried to calculate whether the man sitting in front of her could have ripped someone's head off. He certainly had the bodybuilder physique, but she'd have to search whether human muscles had the force to detach a head. And that would mess up her search history for sure.

"And where were you this evening?" Detective Ledd carried on his questions.

"I was out with the little lady and our son at Sorella's, do you know it? Great Italian just down the road in Omensford. Mention me to the owner, she'll see you right. Look, here, isn't he the spit of me?"

Fi quirked an eyebrow at the chubby face staring out from the Italian leather wallet. If she was uncharitable, she might say that Mr Denzel's kid resembled a pig in a wig, but she wasn't the type to say that…out loud.

"OK, thank you." Larry scribbled on his pad. "Anything else you want to tell us?"

"Only that it's going to cost me a fortune to replace the pumpkins, so the sooner you can get finished up and I can reopen the better."

"Pumpkins?" Fi asked.

He nodded, sending a shockwave across the muscles in his neck. "All of them gone! Destroyed our pumpkin patch display. I tell you, if I find out it's my employees, I'll dock it from their pay. Some of them were real whoppers. I can't figure out how anyone could have moved them without a vehicle, and I've got a strict policy about vehicles near the house during show times – don't want to ruin the ambiance."

"OK, thank you Mr Denzel, we'll be in touch."

Another crippling handshake and he left the room. Detective Ledd turned to Fi. "Come on, I've got something to show you."

Fi followed, scuffing her shoes along the cement floor as Larry led the way out of the cramped office to another room with a large monitor showing shots from all the cameras in the house. Fi gazed at the black and white images of empty rooms with soft grey furniture depicted clearly under the night vision cameras.

"Great, so they can see everything that goes on inside the house. Makes sense, I guess, in case there's any trouble with the actors. No cameras out the back, though," Fi observed as she noted the last employees head out of the front door towards the car park.

"That's not what I wanted to show you..." The detective nodded at the young police officer who pressed some buttons. Fi's face loomed large in one of the squares, frozen in a scream. She narrowed her eyes. The detective smirked at her, his lips twisted into a slash of a smile while the officer tried not to laugh. He pressed play and Fi watched herself scurry through the playroom and into the spider's den.

A flash of light flared for a second and the camera in the stairs went out. Fi swallowed. That would be when she blasted the swinging spider. Another camera picked her and Mort out as they climbed the stairs behind the clown. Mort's high cheekbones were more pronounced on the screens.

"I hope you're studying the rest of the footage so keenly," Fi commented, channelling her best impression of her mother. It didn't work. The detective still looked like he was enjoying himself. She tried a different tactic. "Have it all sent to me asap."

With that, she turned on the heels of her muddy converse trainers and went to find Mort.

# Chapter 21

Fi rearranged the layout of her virtual corkboard again. Cressida's tail whipped on the bed.

*Will you ever stop that incessant tapping?*

"Yeah, yeah, soon."

*You won't be able to investigate anything if you don't get any sleep.*

"I'll come to bed soon, OK?"

Cressida closed her green eyes and curled up on the duvet. Fi rolled her own eyes. Anyone would think that the wyrm was her mother. But how could she be expected to sleep now? She had practically witnessed another murder. Fi stared at the screen.

And properly messed up her date with Mort.

Although it wasn't exactly her fault that they'd stumbled across a corpse.

True to his word, he'd waited for her and driven her back, but finding a body had killed the mood and they'd ended the date with a silent drive back to her house, followed by an awkward kiss goodbye in the car. It was so far from the promise at the beginning of the evening, that it was almost comical. Almost.

She drummed her fingers on the desk. Was it even meant to be? A witch who couldn't control her powers and a…well whatever Mort was. Plus, there was her job. This type of thing could happen at any time, and she'd have to run off and investigate, it wasn't fair to ask someone to wait for her. At least, that's what her ex had said.

She shook her head. Li had wanted too much from her. She should have read the signs when he asked her to choose between online gaming and him.

No brainer really.

She needed her own space and he wanted to smother her, at least that's how it felt. She shuddered, pushing away the memory of her ex. He had no business intruding on her thoughts about Mort…although if the doctor felt the same, it was better to know sooner rather than later.

Fi chewed her lip. Maybe she should blow off their next date for some game time without him so she could get her thoughts straight. She sighed. But she wanted to spend time with Mort, and, by the end of their relationship, she hadn't even wanted to be in the same room as Li.

There. She'd admitted the truth to herself. She hadn't enjoyed being with Li. He was overprotective, scowled at everyone who looked at her and was suspicious of her online persona. Plus, there was that 'more' that he wanted that she just couldn't give him.

She wasn't wired that way and the thought of spending every single waking moment with someone…how could anyone live like that? Not even her sister, Agatha, spent every moment with her husband, and they were so in love it was sickening. Fi let out a loud sigh; she was going to have to talk to Mort.

But it was two in the morning, probably not the best time to call up someone for a conversation about a relationship. Fi pulled a face. Since when had she become someone who wanted to talk about where things were going? That was far too cliché.

She focused on the screen and moved a picture from one corner of the board to another. Better to concentrate on the case at hand.

She searched for O'Riley and wasn't disappointed. Images of him at protests reinforced her idea of him as a fanatical supernatural hater.

He went straight to the top of her suspect list; hated supernaturals – check, hated anything to do with magic – check.

There was the small matter of him being human and not able to rip someone's head off, but she'd figure it out. She jotted down notes on the interviews and something niggled at the back of her mind. Fi tried to concentrate on it, but the thought was elusive and skittered away every time she got close. Something about the interviewees.

Her gaze strayed to the middle of the screen where a large pumpkin sat. How were vegetables important in all this?

An email popped up and she opened it. Sita had sent through the list of beings she had warded against. Fi opened it and read it through, nodding as she took in the creatures and magical beings covered by the ward around the florist's shop.

It was comprehensive and covered everything Fi would expect to see around Omensford: witches, wizards, warlocks, werewolves, fae and even went as far as selkies and hellhounds. That didn't exactly narrow down her investigation.

Fi searched the MLO database for magical creatures not covered by the spell and groaned as the list of over a thousand different supernatural beings popped up, including subsets of each type. One column in the database listed protected characteristics that could form the basis of a discrimination claim.

She read through with interest, who knew that wolf whistling a werewolf was a form of discrimination?

Fi kept scrolling. Maybe a wendigo had roamed through the Cotswolds and cleared the place of pumpkins.

A message popped up in the bottom corner of the screen. She opened it with a smile; Adrock, her closest online friend had logged in. Perfect, just the escape she needed.

Adrock: fancy a game? new skins are out

Fi-zar: nice. what skins?

Adrock: Haunted House!

Fi shuddered. She'd had enough of haunted houses today.

Fi-zar: no thanks. not tonight

Adrock: your loss. anything wrong?

She screwed up her face as she thought. Yes. There was a lot wrong. But not much she could say to her friend.

Fi-zar: just work stuff, got a lot on

Adrock: ouch. i feel you. is it all demons and spirits at halloween?

Fi shook her head at the screen. She'd told her friends about her job at the MLO, but there were so many stereotypes about supernaturals and the obsession with Halloween said more about humans than magical beings. But…maybe Adrock was onto something.

Fi-zar: maybe…got a few things to look into. Thanks for the help

Adrock: ???

Fi-zar: gtg

He sent through a thumbs up. Fi checked the time. Far too late to do anything now so she nudged Cressida to one side of the bed and settled down to sleep, her brain racing with her new plan.

Chapter 22

"Hi Timmy…"

*This won't work.*

Fi ignored the wyrm.

"How dare thou shorten my appellation in such a manner. Thou shouldst quake before me, mortal."

*Good point. Why do you insist on shortening everyone's name?*

"Ri-ight. OK Tim-ey-ass." Fi ignored the wyrm and deliberately emphasised the last syllable of his name. The donkey demon – or should that be demon donkey? – gave a snort. "I need your help."

The donkey pawed at the ground. "I will never aid thee, witch." He turned and cropped at the lawn with his muzzle.

"Not even for a bag of apples?" Fi waved the bag temptingly.

Timaeus raised his head and twitched his nose. Fi took a step forward and held out an apple. He sniffed at it, his warm donkey breath huffing over her palm and Fi allowed herself a small smile. Then the donkey spun round, knocked the apple from her hand and shoved her with his bottom, forcing Fi to step to the side. She swore.

*I told you he wouldn't help. Demons are selfish creatures, only interested in themselves.*

"Completely opposite to familiars then."

*Exactly,* Cressida agreed.

Fi sighed. The sarcasm was lost on the small wyrm. Fi dropped the apples to the ground, where they rolled over the moist grass and took out a bag of sugar lumps.

These were her last attempt to get a demonic donkey to help. And goddess knew that she needed help. Just this morning she'd received a message from Agent Jones, her boss, asking where the report on the pumpkin patch murder was.

Her exact words had been; 'Where the hell is the dzraking report, Blair? I've got the police write ups here; two murders in supernatural circumstances. The Director is breathing down my neck on this. What are you working on? Get me an update. Today.'. It had been a voicemail, so Fi had been spared the need to reply. Instead, she'd sent a text promising an update and saying she was following up on some leads.

One of which stood in front of her, regarding her with deep red eyes that jarred with his long donkey face.

"I suppose these won't work either?" she asked, not hopeful as she jostled the paper bag so a large lump of sugar fell onto her palm.

Timaeus' nose twitched again, and his ears flicked.

"Demons are not permitted to sup on ambrosia." Timaeus eyed her hand.

"It's not ambrosia…"

He looked over his shoulder and regarded Fi with his big red eyes. He came to her and bent his head over her hand. Noisy crunches filled the garden. Fi mimed, "I told you so" at her familiar and looked down at the donkey. She was tempted to rub his velvety ears, but the last time she had tried that, she'd almost lost a finger.

"You like the sugar lumps then?"

Timaeus eyed the brown paper bag.

"Well, if you play nice and help me, I'll give you all the cubes you can eat." She held out another cube to sweeten the deal.

He chomped it, slobbering all over her hand, then licked his lips with a long, pink tongue. "I shall treat with you, mortal. What wouldst thou have me do?"

Chapter 23

*I don't understand why you don't trust my nose.*

Fi sighed. "I do trust you, but he might be able to sense magic that passed your senses by."

The wyrm gave a snort and rearranged herself around Fi's neck. The witch winced as the small animal dug her claws into her skin. Fi tugged on the rope that her mother had helped get round the donkey's thick neck and his pace switched from amble to saunter as they headed to Harris' pumpkin patch.

The old warlock met them at the gate and let them in. He eyed the donkey with a bemused smile. "What's that then?"

"Harris meet Timaeus. Timaeus, this is Harris."

The donkey snorted. Harris went to stroke his ears. "Who's a good boy then?"

"I wouldn't do that if I were you." Fi caught the warlock's hand before he touched the donkey. Timaeus' eyes glowed with a vicious cunning.

"Oh, right, yes, well then. Come on." Harris stomped off over the muddy field and Fi traipsed after him, tugging the donkey with her.

"What manner of place is this?" Timaeus brayed as they picked their way over deep muddy furrows.

"This is a field."

The donkey's nostrils flared.

"I need you to tell me if any demons have been here."

"How dare thou mock me? If I were not trapped in this mule, I would smite thee to dust."

"I'm not mocking you. Some weird stuff has been happening in this town. People's heads being ripped off, pumpkins being stolen. I want to rule out demonic forces. You got trapped in a donkey's body, maybe something else from your realm is here too."

"If any of my fellow demons had come through from our realm, I would have felt the ripple in the cosmos. Thou hast brought me here for nothing. Let us return home."

"Please, Timaeus, can you sense around? Just think of the sugar lumps."

The donkey took a deep breath, his mouth salivating, and he closed his eyes. "I sense the aftermath of magic...."

"What magic?" Fi leaned forward.

"A force of natural magic and lightning."

Fi huffed out a sigh. Harris used magic on his pumpkins for sure, and she was the only witch she knew with anything like lightning powers. The donkey had picked up her aura. She tugged him over to the ditch where they had found Nigel.

"I'll, er, wait 'ere, if you don't mind, Fi. I can't…"

Fi scaled a large mound of mud and placed her hand on Harris' shoulder. "It's alright. I can take it from here and we can find our own way out. Thank you."

The warlock looked relieved, and he tramped his way back to his house, leaving deep footprints in his wake.

Fi returned to the ditch. "And here?"

The ass opened his mouth and Fi got the impression he was breathing in the scene; it was unsettling. She shifted a little, her wellies sucking in the mud, but she stopped herself from backing away from the demon donkey.

"Ah, blood…"

*Demons! All they think about is blood and power.*

Fi tugged on the rope around his neck.

"How much experience have you had with demons?" Fi whispered to her familiar before raising her voice to Timaeus. "Anything else?"

"No new magic here. Now, I believe thou promised me a reward…" The donkey's voice was smooth as silk, but his eyes still had that red tinge.

Fi held out a sugar lump. He stared at her hand.

"Thou insults me with this paltry treat!"

"Take it or leave it, but we've got other places to go so you're not getting the whole bag until we're done."

Fi thought it was amazing how much disdain a donkey could get into such a normally placid face, but he crunched up the sugar lump and allowed himself to be led back across the field and into town.

They stopped at the florist shop, but other than a couple of sneezes from Cressida, which charred a small rosebush, there was nothing out of the ordinary there either.

"Awww, a donkey, how quaint! Can I stroke him?"

"Er, best not," Fi told the tourist. Timaeus flattened his ears against his head and bared his yellowed teeth. "He's in a bad mood."

"Oh now, I handle critters like this all the time on the ranch back home," his American accent held a hint of scorn.

"Not like this one," Fi muttered under her breath.

Timaeus stomped his hooves on the ground and narrowed his red eyes. The tourist finally realised something was amiss and backed off just as Agatha's pick-up truck pulled up outside the florists.

"Did someone order a ride?" Agatha leaned over and beamed out of the window.

"Took your time," Fi grumbled as she went around back and fiddled with the tailgate.

"The correct response is: 'Thank you, Agatha, you are the best sister in the world and I'm lucky to have you.' Some of us have other things to do with our time. You're lucky I wasn't at work, or you'd be riding that demon to the other side of the Cotswolds." Agatha joined her at the back of the truck and pulled down the door with practised ease.

"Thank you, Agatha."

"Not at all." Her sister didn't even notice her gritted teeth. "Anything for my beloved sister."

"Knock it off and help me load up this donkey."

Chapter 24

After much swearing from Fi, some choice curses from Timaeus, sarcastic comments from Cressida, and several exclamations of "Fudge!" from Agatha, the donkey was safely ensconced in the back of the truck, and they were on their way to the second murder site.

"So, what are you hoping to find? Are we going to catch some perps?"

Cressida snorted a laugh.

"We're not in a cop movie, Agatha, and I'm hoping that Timmy back there can sense some magic that can give me a lead."

"Sure, sure, but I'm taking a weapon just in case."

Fi rolled her eyes as her sister swung the car out to overtake a lorry. "The murder's already happened, you don't need a weapon."

"Yeah, well, after what happened last Halloween, I'm not taking any chances with our safety."

Fi's mind travelled back to the previous Halloween, when an elderly witch had been killed and she'd been accused of murder. It hadn't had a happy ending. She flexed her fingers. She had killed someone with her power.

Sure, they had been about to kill her, Agatha, and Cressida with killer bees, but still, it showed how destructive she was and how quickly she could kill if things got out of control, not like her sister's nature magic that matched her nurturing personality. Somewhere among the memory, a malign thought lingered; what if Fi's power matched her nature and she was a killer?

Another question pulled Fi from her melancholy musings. "What weapon have you got?"

Agatha grinned and rummaged in the compartment between the two front seats. She pulled her arm free, brandishing a pair of secateurs. The blade gleamed wickedly in the red glow of a traffic light they were stopped at. The light turned green, Agatha dropped the tool and the pick-up raced forward.

"What are you going to do with them? A bit of landscaping?"

"Don't be ridiculous. I'll prune any killers down to size."

"Not planning an am*bush* then?"

"Maybe I'll use some *bush*ido."

Fi snorted. "I'd join you, but I'm *bush*whacked."

"Oooo, good one. Then we can sec it to them." Fi frowned at her sister. Agatha raised her eyebrows. "You know, like sock it to them but sec it because they're secateurs."

"Nope, that was terrible. You should use that if we do find the killer though, they'll be so busy groaning at your bad puns, we'll be able to catch them easily."

Agatha grinned back at Fi. "We're here, and I'm still taking them with me." She hopped out of the truck and wedged the secateurs in the back pocket of her patched jeans.

Fi rolled her eyes and got out of the car.

*Why is your sister so excited?* Cressida asked, jumping down beside Fi.

"She doesn't get out much."

Fi joined Agatha at the back of the vehicle and unhooked the tailgate. Timaeus jumped down. He might have intended a majestic leap to the ground, but being in the form of a donkey, he landed hard and overbalanced, hitting his muzzle onto the soft ground.

"Ouch, ten points for effort though," Fi said. Agatha elbowed her in the side and helped Timaeus up. His nose was covered in a thick layer of brown mud. "I hope you can still sense magic."

"Foolish witch. It is my essence that can sense magic, not the mere snout of an animal. This muck is a mere annoyan-brouhaaa!" It looked like Timaeus' body had other thoughts about the mud because he shook his head, brayed loudly, took two steps backwards and wiped his nose on Fi's coat.

"Brilliant," she grumbled.

"That garment is so odious, I know not how you can tell it is any filthier."

She noticed the sly look on Timaeus' face. "You chose me on purpose, didn't you? Agatha was right there next to you, and you walked backwards."

"A coincidence, mortal."

Fi narrowed her eyes. "Just do your thing or I'll eat the sugar myself." She crunched a cube loudly for emphasis.

Agatha took his rope lead in one hand, brandished her gardening tool in the other and led Timaeus along the path towards the haunted house while Fi paused to try to wipe the mud off her coat.

*Why must you be so uncouth?*

"He started it."

*I can see I still have much to teach you in the way of manners and how a young witch should behave.*

"Don't you start," Fi scowled as she caught up with her sister.

"It looks a lot less impressive in the daytime." Agatha sounded disappointed.

"Not planning on wetting yourself then?"

Her sister blushed a bright red. "I just screamed, that's all. You have kids, then you can talk to me about pelvic floors."

Fi blanched. Kids? No thank you. "Alright, keep your panties on, it was a joke."

"Ha. Ha."

Fi turned to the donkey. "OK Timmy – I mean, Timaeus, do your thing."

The demon donkey walked around in a circle then shook his head. Fi yanked his rope, pulling him along the path, closer to the house. A dog walker stared at them. Agatha pocketed her bladed tool.

"Hi there, just taking our donkey for a walk."

The man and his dog hurried on, head down against the wind.

"Ouch."

"What happened?" Fi spun round; hands raised, ready to attack. Electricity sparked in her palms.

Agatha smiled sheepishly and sucked on her finger. "I cut myself."

Fi gave her sister a look that caused Agatha to stick her tongue out. Fi turned back to the donkey. "How about here?"

Agatha prowled around with her uninjured hand resting on the sharpened secateurs in her pocket. Fi ignored her and focused on the donkey sniffing around on the path.

"Nothing. I can sense the same magic as before, nature and lightning. And a vampire was here."

"Yeah, he jumped out at us…" The niggle at the back of her brain reappeared and this time it didn't disappear. A vampire was strong enough to rip someone's head off. It looked like she had a new top suspect.

## Chapter 25

After bundling Timaeus back into the pick-up truck and safely depositing him back in her mother's garden, Fi called up the detective. Two emails later and Fi was working her way through the list of interviewees from the Haunted House.

She scanned it twice but couldn't recall interviewing the vampire and none of Larry's notes made her think that he'd spoken to the supernatural without her. So now, she cross-checked the interviewees against the list of employees working that night.

She huffed out a sigh. It was manual work that could be easily automated but populating a spreadsheet and writing the macro to do it would take longer than doing it by hand. She would have been tempted to do it on the computer anyway if the heavy feeling in her stomach, like a rock sitting in her midriff, wasn't telling her that the vampire was already long gone.

"Yes!"

Cressida jumped and flicked out her forked tongue in irritation.

*What happened?*

She double checked. The paperwork showed that a Valentine Lapell had signed in for his shift but hadn't signed out and he wasn't on the interviewee list. "I've got our vampire. Now to find him."

She searched on social media but wasn't too surprised not to find anything. Vampires had long lives and weren't always up to speed with the latest technologies, plus many of them tried to blend in with humans and that meant frequent identity changes. Not ideal candidates for cyber stalking.

Fi logged onto her work profile and checked the Magical Liaison Office's database. She struck lucky; he had registered with the MLO, and there was an address with a phone number. Fi dialled it. No answer. Of course not. He was a vampire; the stories about dying in sunlight were true. So, she had time to kill while she waited for nightfall.

On a whim, she called the Haunted House. A chirpy voice answered.

"Hello, Denzel's holiday experiences, how may I help you?"

"I was wondering who was on tonight?"

"Who is this?"

"Fiona Blair. I was there last night, and I wondered if it would be the same actors."

"Don't worry, Miss Blair, all our actors are professionally trained but the experience does vary slightly from day to day."

This wasn't working. "I'm one of the officers who was at the scene of the…crime. I need to speak to Valentine Lapell. Is he working tonight?"

"We don't usually disclose information about our actors…"

"Please. You could save a life."

A long silence, and then, "I'm sorry Ms Blair, unless I can see your badge, I can't give out that information."

The lady was loyal to her company's policies. "You could call me back through work, that'd confirm that I'm legitimate."

"I'm sorry Ms Blair, I really don't have the time…"

"OK, could you leave a message for him?"

"Of course."

"Could you tell him to listen to his voicemail and call me back urgently?"

"Certainly, I'll leave that with our front desk ready for tonight. Will there be anything else?"

"No, thank you." Fi hung up, a big smile spreading across her face. The receptionist had let slip that he'd be working tonight. She stretched, content with her work.

Then she scowled as she remembered; she still had to write that stupid report.

Chapter 26

Fi avoided meeting the protestors' eyes as they marched around in a small circle, back in their place next to the ticket booth. She flashed her ID at the lady on the gate, today wearing a tall witch's hat as a token effort at dressing up. The woman glanced at it, flicked her eyes to Fi and nodded.

Cressida made a small noise of disgust from her perch on Fi's shoulder.

"Pumpkin patch is still closed to the public, if that's where you're headed."

Fi nodded back. It wasn't where she was going, but the ticket lady didn't need to know that. Fi took her time meandering up the path to the Haunted House.

*Is that what people think witches are nowadays? Black hats and lace? Shocking.*

"It's supposed to be sexy."

*Sexy?* The wyrm spat out the word.

Fi stepped to one side to allow the zombie to shuffle past, arms outstretched. He tried hard, with his best groans, but soon gave up when he saw she wasn't scared. He moved on to the small group of teenagers behind her, still moaning.

*Why does a witch need to be sexy? Isn't it enough to be a strong independent magic user who can look after themselves. That should be the role model, not,* she looked back over her shoulder, *whatever that is.*

"Huh, I never thought of it like that."

*If I ever see you dressed up with such blatant disrespect for witchkind, I will burn your clothes to ashes.*

"Good to know."

Fi slowed again when she reached the gravestones looming from the mist. Now she was ready for it, she could see the fog machine hidden behind a large wonky cross.

"Bevare!" The vampire sprang up from his hiding place in full regalia.

"Knock it off, Valentine."

He blinked at her, confused. "Do I know you? Oh, you were here the other night, right? Come back for more?"

She stepped forward and gripped his wrist loosely. "I just want to talk, let's step behind that gravestone." With her free hand, she flashed him her badge.

His jaw tensed and he pulled free. Fi had to act. Vampires were fast and this could be her only chance. She released a blast of magic at him as soon as he started to pull away.

He landed on his back twenty feet away. "Ouch."

"I'm so sorry, are you OK?" Fi knelt on the damp grass, looking for injuries. His frilly shirt had a large scorch mark on it, and she could see the burning flesh underneath, red and blistered from her magic. She winced at the damage she'd cause. "Er, how can I help?"

"You don't," he said pointedly.

At least she hadn't stopped his heart, although she wasn't sure if vampire hearts beat. They were dead, weren't they? She rubbed her forehead. She didn't remember much vampire lore. Looking down at Valentine's bright red eyes, that seemed like a massive oversight on her part.

"I just want to talk."

"Then why did you blast me? You've ruined this shirt; we have to pay for damages you know."

"You were trying to run."

"Yeah, well, I don't need the trouble. I've got a good job here; I want to keep it so I can save up enough to get to London. Not all vampires have centuries worth of money hidden away, you know."

"Just talk to me and you can get right back to work."

"Fine. You can take your hand off me you know."

"If I do that, you'll be a mile away before I can blink."

He grinned, showing his fangs. "Maybe, but I won't run. Vampire's honour."

Fi eyed his mouth, raised one eyebrow, and kept her hand on his shoulder. She focused on his slicked down hair to avoid looking directly into his eyes as a half-remembered thought pushed its way to the front of her mind; vampires could hypnotise people and make them believe anything they wanted. "Tell me about last night."

"What do you want to know?" Valentine sounded resigned. Fi risked a glance at his face. Something flickered there, was it anger or disappointment? Then it was gone, his pale face went blank, and he stared at his feet.

"Why didn't you stay to be interviewed?"

"I told you; I didn't want the trouble. The minute something goes wrong, they blame the vampires. As soon as I smelled all that blood, I went."

"Did you go and look?"

He shuddered and shook his head.

"Why not?"

The vampire gave her a look. "Lots of blood."

"And?"

His voice lowered, soft, like a cat's purr. "It's like…a craving, right. We need blood to live, not sure why but our bodies crave it, we can eat other food, sure, but blood is what we need. Now I get by with the animal stuff they sell in the butchers, but human blood, that's like…imagine the best thing you've ever tasted. Hold that in your mind."

Fi pictured her neighbour's chocolate cake, goddess but it was delicious; decadent icing oozed over its surface and inside it was the perfect balance of sponge and filling with enough moistness to melt in the mouth. She could almost smell the rich, chocolatey aroma; not too sweet but not exactly bitter. A slice of that cake with a cup of Goblin Blend coffee was as close to perfection as she could imagine. Saliva gathered in her mouth, and she swallowed.

"You're picturing it, aren't you? I can tell," Valentine continued, "Now, compare everything else to that, it's just not the same, is it? For vampires, it's a hundred times worse because we're programmed to want blood and whatever this virus is inside us, it wants to spread to other humans. Even if we've already fed and aren't hungry, we must constantly control our urges, so we don't give in to temptation. Like now, you're so close to me and I can hear your heartbeat, see the artery in your neck pulsing. All it would take is one bite and I'd be drunk on the exquisite taste of you."

She nodded along. Vampires were so brave to fight temptation all the time, it was sad that they had to suffer so much. If only there was a way she could help this one…maybe if she offered him her blood, he could ease the cravings that bound him so tightly. She leaned forward.

*What are you doing? Shake it off! You are a powerful witch, not a weak human. Do not succumb to his powers.*

Cressida dug her claws into Fi's skin to emphasise the point. The witch blinked. What spell had the youthful looking vampire cast on her? She allowed a small shock of electricity to pulse from her hand. He winced again and when he next spoke, his voice lost some of its lulling qualities.

"I wouldn't alright, I've fed this week, and I told you, I'm in control. But it's like balancing on a knife edge. There's this force that wants to break free and give in, and you have to fight it. All the time.

"It's why so few vampires are made. So that's why I didn't go to investigate. I can resist humans most of the time, but freshly spilled blood…" He shuddered. "I didn't want to risk getting swept up in bloodlust."

It all sounded so reasonable. Fi scowled. "But why didn't you tell anyone?"

"I thought about phoning it in, but…if anyone found out it was me that made the call," he shrugged, "it's just not worth it."

"Someone died!"

"And I'm sorry about that, and frankly a little surprised no one heard the scuffle…"

"You heard it?!" More magic leaked from her hand into the vampire. He flinched.

"Cut it out with the shocks!" He clocked the look on the witch's face. "Please."

Fi nodded and forced her power down. She hadn't meant to hurt him that time, but the thought that he'd heard the struggle and hadn't helped had caused her to lose control.

He took a deep breath. "I heard a slithering sound, then a shout, then fighting noises. I thought one of the guests might have gone a bit too far with an actor. That happens sometimes. But then I smelled the blood." The vampire's eyes turned a more vibrant shade of red. "And I decided to scarper."

"Anything else you can tell me?"

"It wasn't a vampire that killed him, that's all I know."

"How do you know that?" Fi looked at him sharply.

"Because a vampire wouldn't have wasted so much fresh blood."

# Chapter 27

Fi swallowed to hide her discomfort at the casual way Valentine had described the killing. "OK, anything else?"

He shook his head and his eyes dimmed to a more muted rust colour. Fi stood and offered him her hand. He placed his cold palm in hers but put no pressure on her as he stood.

The vampire brushed himself down and said, "You're…not going to report me, are you?"

Fi's brow furrowed. "I'll have to mention you in the report, to rule you out as a suspect."

He groaned.

"It'll be fine."

"It won't be fine." He sounded forlorn. "This is how it starts. I should never have registered with the Magical Liaison Office. First, someone finds out you're a real vampire, then they come with stakes. Then I've got to move out before they set fire to my home."

"It won't come to that."

"A real vampire? Hey! They've got a real vampire here!"

Fi looked up and saw O'Riley shouting and waving his arms, a puff of mist came from the vape inhaler clutched in his sweaty palm.

Valentine put his head in his hands. "It's already started."

"Couldn't you sense him? Aren't you meant to be able to hear heartbeats?" Fi hissed.

The vampire's eyes flared bright red again. "Don't blame me! You're the one who accosted me! I wasn't exactly focused on other people when you hit me with your magic."

Fi stood and squared her shoulders. Valentine trailed behind her, his head down as if resigned to his fate.

O'Riley had drawn a small crowd. Unfortunately for him, they were all thrill seekers come to the Haunted House and his cries of 'Vampire!' were met with drawls of 'Cool!' and 'Can I get a picture?' as the patrons craned their necks to see the supernatural.

Fi nudged Valentine in the side. "Looks like your adoring fans await. I'll deal with the protestors."

She grabbed O'Riley's upper arm and perp walked him back to the ticket booth. Once there, she released her grip, and he rubbed his arm.

"Bloody fascist. We've got a right to protest, you know."

Fi tilted her head to one side and pretended to consider that. "Maybe…but not on private property. Does Mr Denzel know you're here?"

"What does he care?"

"He might care if you're upsetting his customers and his staff."

"You don't scare me."

Cressida bared her teeth at the human and let out a hiss.

"Well, I should. I'm a Magical Liaison Office agent and you're harassing a supernatural; that's discrimination against a protected characteristic. And you're trespassing on private property…" She counted the offences off on her fingers as she went.

"How do you know Denzel didn't let us on here?"

Fi raised one eyebrow. "Oh, I'm sure he'll side with me on this. Especially if he doesn't want an MLO investigation into cultural appropriation on his hands."

*Nice touch.* There was a hint of admiration in the wyrm's voice.

"It's a bloody conspiracy!"

"No, Mr O'Riley, it's the law." Fi was proud of how calm and assured she sounded. "Do you want me to carry on citing misdemeanours until I decide to arrest you, or do you want to leave now?"

"I'll get back at you for this, it's not right, not right at all. Why do you side with them, those unnaturals?" He spat on the ground.

Fi gave a slow smile and allowed her power to settle on her hands until they glowed with a blue light. Her hair spread slowly as it responded to her magic, frizzing out until it framed her head with a white halo. "Mr O'Riley, I am one of those 'unnaturals' as you called us, and you would do well to leave before my patience runs out."

*Bravo! Well done!* Cressida's praise rang in her ears.

"You'll be sorry for this!" he shouted. Fi took a step forward and he scrambled backwards, tripping over his cardboard sign. "Come on, Delores, let's go."

Fi smiled as the protestors fled across the car park to their ancient van. At least that was a job well done; they wouldn't be back to bother the Haunted House or Valentine.

## Chapter 28

Fi's eyes glazed over, and she pulled a face. Was there anything worse than writing a report? She'd already completed the simple fields on the Incident Form, like Name of Officer and Date of Incident. Description of Incident was simple too. There weren't many ways to describe a headless body.

She'd linked the incident at Harris' farm with the one at the Haunted House and attached copies of the autopsy reports that Robbie had sent on to her and the detective.

She'd also added the break-in at the florists as a suspicious incident and linked that, not that there was any evidence to support her theory apart from missing pumpkins. But Sita was a wizard, and that meant she fell under the Magical Liaison Office's protection, which meant she got an incident report. Fi saved Sita's list of creatures covered by her warding spell as an attachment.

She took a small amount of pleasure from writing up the incident with O'Riley; harassing a supernatural, trespassing, threatening an agent. In the conclusion box, she'd written that she'd rather anti-climatically let him off with a warning. But at least he was in the database.

Now she tapped at her own virtual corkboard. She still needed to ask her friend Maxi about getting the software onto the MLO drive, maybe someone else would find it useful, plus it would mean Agent Jones could see her progress and wouldn't chase these stupid reports…except then Agent Jones could see her progress. Which amounted to a big pile of nothing, if she was honest.

Reluctantly, she moved O'Riley down from her top suspect. Fi couldn't see how he would have the strength to rip off a head when she'd been able to manhandle him away from the vampire. And Valentine was out too. He might have the strength to do it, but vampires didn't kill that way; they didn't have too, and why waste a free meal? Nope, vampires weren't the answer.

And neither were demons, according to Timaeus. Of course, he could be lying…demons weren't exactly known for being truthful. Or did they always speak the truth? She rubbed her eyes. This was going to take more than a computer search to figure out. With a sigh, she pushed back her ergonomic chair and moaned.

*Will you be quiet?*

"Sorry, Cress, just trying to solve a double homicide here. But if your sleep is more important…"

The wyrm hissed at her. *Maybe a change of scenery will do you good, help you solve the case.*

"And help you sleep?"

Cressida flicked her tail. *A welcome side effect.*

"Fine, I'd better check the library anyway." Fi left the small animal to her slumber and descended the stairs to the library. She was at the threshold when Effie caught her sleeve.

"Fi, you are making good progress with your case, aren't you?"

"Yes, I mean, I've hit a bit of a stumbling block, but nothing too major." Just the small matter of having no idea and no leads.

"Only, the concert is coming up and Cirian's a bit nervous about all these killings. He didn't get in from his nature walk until the early hours and he needs to be in the right head space to perform."

"Right. Yep. I'm on it."

"And, I hate to bring it up, with the murders and everything…"

"Yes?"

"Someone's stolen the decorations for his concert!"

"Not really my area…"

"I know, sorry to bother you."

"Wait!" Fi stopped Effie as she walked away. "Were they pumpkins? The decorations?"

"Yes, I think it was rather pumpkin heavy on the set. I did say that it was a bit obvious, but…" She shrugged one shoulder.

"And are there security cameras?"

"On the common? I don't think so. But Cirian said he thought he saw something at one of his rehearsals."

"Really? That's brilliant! I mean, I should talk to him about it."

"So, you'll help?"

"Of course."

"I knew you would," Effie clapped her hands together.

"Er, Effie, you sent a postcard that mentioned the case…"

"Yes?"

"Did you happen to see anything in one of your visions?"

"Ah. No, sorry dear, I saw that you would have a case and there was something important in your past, but nothing else. I'm sure you can solve it quickly though." Effie patted her on the arm. "Now, I must speak to your mother about the sound system arrangements for the concert."

Fi kept her smile plastered on until Effie walked into the kitchen, then she allowed her face to fall. Hearing footsteps, she looked up and turned her lips up again as she saw Cirian. She had to look in control at least.

"Effie said you might have seen something strange at a rehearsal."

The elf was silent for so long that Fi went to repeat the question when he spoke in a soft, lilting voice.

"I didn't see anything, exactly. More a feeling of something large and I heard this strange thumping and slithering, like something big moving through the trees." He shrugged. "Sorry, it's not much."

"Was this before or after all the pumpkins went missing?"

"Before. And I had this strange sensation I was being watched the whole time. The set was there when I left, but when I came back this morning, the whole thing was ruined and not a pumpkin to be seen."

"OK, thanks. I'll look into it."

"I'm not sure the concert can go ahead with all this theft and murder in the village."

"No! It'll be fine. You just focus on your voice. Leave everything else to me." She couldn't let Effie or Steve down and now Cirian looked at her with those sparkling eyes. They were all counting on her. She would find the culprit and bring them to justice and get Omensford its Halloween concert.

"Effie trusts you, so I do too. I shall go and meditate to make sure I am in the right frame of mind for the concert. Thank you, Fiona."

"No problem." She kept her bright smile on until he was back in the kitchen before she slumped against a wall. Why did she have to promise she could solve this? She had nothing. With a sigh, she pushed open the door to the library. This was her last lead.

The electric candles came on by themselves, bathing the library in a warm glow, and she stood in the middle of the room, digging her feet into the deep pile rug for moral support.

"OK, library. This is a weird request, but I need to know if we have anything on supernaturals or demons who decapitate people by ripping their heads off." She thought for a moment.

"And anything on pumpkins and why someone might take them, a lot of pumpkins, I mean."

There was a long silence, as if the room was thinking. Fi waited. And waited. Then she let her shoulders slump.

"OK, well thank you for looking…"

She turned to go when the rustling started, like wings fluttering together. Fi knew by now that it was the pages of the books as the library worked its magic. "Thank you," she whispered as books started to creep out of their positions to the very edge of the shelves.

She collected them one by one until she carried five volumes in her slender hands. She placed them gently on the low coffee table and perched on the edge of the large Chesterfield sofa.

Fi reached for the first one, a recipe book on catering for large covens. She flipped through the pages and there were indeed several recipes that needed pumpkins: pumpkin soup, pumpkin cake, pumpkin pie. Fi huffed and set it to one side. She doubted that someone had taken a field's worth of pumpkins for a gigantic soup.

The rest of the books looked more ominous, with curling gold lettering printed on dark leather and the sense of age in their yellowed pages. Fi recognised the tattooed cover of a book on demons. She picked it up and pushed down the disgust she felt at touching the cover. It felt no different to other leather-bound books, but that tattoo, well let's just say that animals don't normally have tattoos like that.

She turned the pages delicately and leaned back as she took in the detailed pictures, as if distance would make them less disturbing. Demons were not known for being nice and every other page had an illustration of what happened to humans who messed with them alongside pictures of forms that demons commonly took.

Fi's thoughts turned to her encounter with Timaeus when he'd tried to break through the barrier between the demon world and this one, his demonic cloud had been bad enough but some of these were almost comical in how horrifying they were. One look at this book would make George Romero take a step back and say "Now, hang on a minute, this is too far."

Fi forced herself to go through the entire book, but the illustrations showed that demons preferred hearts and other internal organs. While they might drink from cups made from human skulls, it didn't look like they had much use for entire heads, except to eat the brains. She made a note of a couple that found brains a particular delicacy then set that book aside.

The next volume was bound in black lettering and had the words *Tribal Rituals from Around the World* stamped on the front. This book had an index spanning a dozen pages at the back and Fi ran her finger down the page, searching for anything about heads.

Heads; Celtic culture, Heads; drinking vessels, Heads; shrunken, Heads; trophy.

None of that seemed promising, but she looked them all up in turn.

Yes, the Celts decapitated their enemies and had some sort of cult where they took heads as trophies, but they used blades to separate the head from the body, not brute force, and there were tribes and religions that shrank heads for various purposes, but that took time and care and didn't gel with what Fi had seen at the murder scenes. She was no better off than before. The other two books didn't have much to add, and she sank back on the sofa and stared up at the ceiling. She was missing something.

Effie had told her to look to her past to solve this case…well that could mean anything. Her troublesome time at school before she learned to damp down her powers, her dead-end jobs as tech support consultants, her more recent escapades solving murders in the Cotswolds, but all those killers had been apprehended and were dead, or, in the case of Timaeus, trapped in a donkey's body where the worst he could do was bite someone's hand off.

Her phone rang, giving a welcome interruption to her swirling thoughts. Detective Ledd's voice rang through the speaker.

"Any leads on your end?"

"I'm working on it. You?"

"Nothing yet." A long pause. "Did you speak to the werewolves?"

"For the last time, it's not a werewolf!" Fi hung up and said a rude word at the disconnected phone. It rang in her hand, making her jump. Speaking of werewolves.

"Hi Steve."

"Hi Fi, I know you're busy with work, but I could really use your help down here. The coffee machine is still on the fritz and we're so close to opening day."

"Sure, I'll come straight over." Fi closed the book. It wasn't like she had made any progress here. She went upstairs to get a jacket; helping Steve was a welcome distraction from the dead-end research and the bloody MLO incident reports.

# Chapter 29

"Thank goodness you came! I've been having nightmares about this wretched machine and it's spilling over into my baking – last night, I used salt instead of sugar in my chocolate cake. I nearly poisoned Glen!"

"Calm down, Steve…"

"Calm down? Calm down! Do you know how much work there is to do?"

Fi took in the café; not a thing looked out of place. "Well, you've finished the mural…"

"Yes, the mural's done, but what about the rest of it? I'm working by myself while you're off doing your things. I've got to iron the tablecloths, rearrange the displays, and bake all the cakes and bread…"

"You could order in the bread…"

Steve shot her a look that told her exactly what he thought of that idea. "And this stupid machine still isn't working. I've turned it off and on again so many times, it's a wonder the plug isn't broken."

"I'll have a look, but computers are more my speed…"

"Effie said you could fix it!"

"I said I'll take a look; now why don't you take a deep breath and make us both a hot drink from the kettle?"

Steve closed his hazel eyes and inhaled deeply three times. When he opened his eyes again, they were less wild. He smoothed down his shaggy hair. "Sorry about that, I lost my cool for a minute there. You focus on the machine, I'll make the drinks and get on with the displays."

Fi smiled reassuringly at him and then shifted her gaze to the silver monster sitting defiantly on the counter. "OK, Belissimo Coffee 2000, let's go."

The witch tried the tested on and off method, leaving a thirty second interval before she turned it back on again. Sometimes that was all it took. But not this time.

The machine dribbled boiling water through one of its pipes, managing to miss the drip tray entirely. Fi swore and turned it back off. Ignoring the small puddle of water, she tightened every joint she could find.

Steve placed a cup on the counter next to the silver machine. Fi stopped her tinkering and took a sip of coffee gratefully.

She eyed the plain mug. "Did you know that the poet Byron had a cup made from a human skull?"

Steve stared at her. Maybe skulls weren't great small talk, but that was what researching head cults got you. What had her life come to when she thought it was socially acceptable to mention bones in casual conversation?

"Anyway, I've tightened everything up, so let's try again."

She tipped some beans into the grinder and pressed a button. They held their breath as the blades whirred round, then ground to a halt. Fi whacked it with the flat of her hand and the grinder cranked into life again.

"Must have been a loose connection," she smiled.

Next up, she pressed the coffee powder into the sump and attached it to the hot water dispenser. She selected a button with a beep and waited. Nothing happened. She tried the flat of the hand trick again but that dislodged the sump and coffee powder hit the floor in a small cloud, where it mixed with the spilled water.

Well, she had made coffee, but not in a conventional way. With a huff, she bent closer to check the dispenser.

Her phone buzzed in her pocket, causing her to jerk upright and hit her head on the machine. A trickle of her magic sank into the machine, and it sparked dangerously. Both Fi and Steve backed away as the sparks continued. The coffee maker gave a small whirr followed by a grinding noise and then was quiet.

"Is it OK?" asked Steve.

"I think so…" Fi eyed the machine, but it wasn't smoking or in pieces, so that was good. She approached it cautiously and tried a button. Nothing happened. She swore, now she'd really broken it. With a shake of her head, she checked her phone and clicked on the email notification. The video footage was through. She played it on her phone, but the screen was too small to see anything.

"Sorry, Steve. Got to go. You should go home too, get some sleep. It's late. Everything'll be fine, just leave it turned off and I'll look at it soon, promise."

She ignored the dismay on the werewolf's face and raced out of the door.

# Chapter 30

Back in front of her computer, Fi watched the video footage that Detective Ledd had sent through. She squinted at the grainy screen as herself and other guests walked through the Haunted House.

The detective had been good enough to extract a clip of her reactions to the scares in the house and attach that as a separate file when he'd sent the email and he'd copied in Agent Jones as well as the whole of his team. Brilliant.

Detective Ledd had included a message saying that Denzel was adding security cameras outside his attraction. Too little, too late for Trevor though. She attached the file to her incident report and then opened the other clip.

It took her a moment to register what she was looking at, then she recognised Omensford High Street. So, this was the footage from the florist robbery. It was even grainier than the previous file. She squinted and leaned in, her nose almost pressed against her gaming monitor as she tried to make out the different shops, then the screen went black.

Fi's brow furrowed as a huge shape passed the camera and slithered down the High Street. Long tentacles thrashed out, destroying the display outside the Town Hall. The monster paused outside Sita's shop for long moments, then disappeared out of view.

What on earth was that thing?

Fi watched the clip again and paused it at the moment when it was closest to the camera. She squinted, trying to bring the blurry image into focus.

*Have you found something?* Cressida hopped up onto her lap and rested her front legs on the desk.

"What do you make of this?"

The small wyrm flicked her tongue at the screen. *It's a blob.*

"The picture isn't clear, but I bet this is the thing that murdered everyone and look. It stopped at Sita's, so maybe it took the pumpkins too."

*But what is it?*

"No idea." Fi frantically searched for tentacles in the MLO database. "Do you think a kraken could live this far from the sea?"

Cressida gave the witch a look.

"OK, probably not a kraken…but if it's something from the sea, maybe it's lost." She typed her theory into the incident report and submitted it. Better keep Agent Jones updated.

*How are you going to find it?*

"No idea." Fi moved her search to the internet and brought up an aerial map of the town. "It was heading in this direction…maybe it's living not too far from here."

*Where is Harris' farm and the Haunted House on that map?*

"Cressida, you're a genius."

The wyrm preened. *I know.*

Fi dropped pins in the two locations and another on the High Street before adding a fourth to the common where Cirian's stage was set up ready for the concert. She traced the skewed trapezium with a finger.

Where could something that large hide during the day? Her gaze landed on a likely spot. "Maybe it's hiding out in these woods…"

*How are you going to catch it?*

"No idea. But I know someone who can help."

# Chapter 31

"Alright, alright, I'm coming." Agatha put down her copy of Gardener's Weekly and strode to the front door. She pulled it open to find her sister standing on the front step, her familiar curled around her shoulders. "Fi? What are you doing here?"

"Do you have any pumpkins?"

"Pumpkins? Of course I do, I'm going in for best in show at the Tri-Village Halloween Fete again. And this year, I've got it in the bag. It's almost as big as last year's. I upgraded the greenhouse–"

"Great, great, only… I need to borrow it."

"Excuse me?"

"You know the murders…"

"Yes."

"And the pumpkins taken in town…"

"Yes." Agatha's voice was slower this time, taking two syllables to say the word.

"I've got a lead, but I need a pumpkin."

Agatha considered this. Indecision strummed through her; she wanted to help her little sister, but this was her prize pumpkin. After a long moment, she nodded. "OK, but I'm coming too."

"What? No. It's too dangerous."

Agatha arched an eyebrow. "Too dangerous? I helped you with Goody Winships' murderer, and she was a crazy witch in command of a gazillion killer bees."

"But this is big, Aggy. It's huge. Literally. And I don't even know what type of monster it is."

"Even more reason for me to go with you. I'll be your back-up. Besides, you're not taking my pumpkin without me."

Agatha crossed her arms. She could see the internal warring going on inside her sister as she weighed up how much she needed the pumpkin.

"You're not even dressed," said Fi.

Agatha looked down at her flannel trousers. "What do you mean?"

"You're in your pyjamas."

"They're lounge wear. Just give me a second to speak to Neville and I'll meet you round the back." Agatha went to shut the door then paused. "Oh, and watch out for Cluck Norris, he's feeling a bit feisty today, I think it's the new feed."

She shut the door this time, ignoring her sister's eye roll and grabbed her thick jacket. "Neville, I'm going out for a bit."

Her husband looked up from the TV and paused the recorded episode of Countdown. "Going anywhere nice?"

"Fi needs some help, and you know the trouble she can get into without me."

"Hmmm."

"What does that mean?"

"Just…she is an adult, and an MLO agent, she can take care of herself."

"But can she take care of my pumpkin?"

Neville's brows drew together quizzically but he didn't ask the question that bubbled to his lips. Agatha bent over and kissed him on the forehead. "Don't worry, I'll be back soon. Make sure Bea reads you some of her schoolbook before bed so you can write it in the reading record."

"Yes, dear."

"And there's a shepherd's pie in the oven, it'll be ready in about ten minutes."

"Yes, dear."

"And stop saying 'yes, dear' like that."

"Yes, dear."

Agatha's lips curved into a smile at Neville's teasing tone, and she shook her head at her husband. "Love you."

"Love you more."

With a final kiss and a cuddle with her daughter, who protested at the interruption to her game of knights and dragons, Agatha headed out of the back door to her garden.

She inhaled deeply as she stepped outside, her smile broadening unconsciously.

As always, this first step was like entering another world, a private haven of flowers and plants that spoke to her on an elemental level. She could feel the vibrancy in the ground, the richness of the earth and the love of her plants. An errant rambling rose caught her attention.

She tsked at it and touched the late-blooming flower with one finger. It twisted back to the circular metal climbing frame and joined the other stems winding around the frame.

"That's better." Agatha smiled at the roses, her expert eye roving over the blossoms for signs of blight. The weather had chilled, and mist crept in with the setting sun. She'd have to set up her frost protection spells soon, or the flowers would be ravaged by the cold.

An aggressive squawk drew her attention from the flowerbed, and she turned to see Fi kicking wildly at the large rooster that patrolled her garden.

"Stop upsetting him!"

"He's upsetting me. I just walked over to the greenhouse, and he attacked!"

"You're in his territory."

"Get over here and get him under control or we'll be having roasted cockerel for dinner!"

Agatha rolled her eyes and joined her sister on the other side of the garden. With a practised grab, she snatched Cluck Norris up and tucked him under one arm. He glowered at Fi and struck out with his clawed feet.

"Calm down, Cluck. Away with you." Agatha walked to the chicken coop and dropped the cockerel inside, where he continued to glare at Fi, and he stabbed at the wire fence with his beak. "I don't know what's got into him."

"He's a demon in chicken form. Now, come on, Aggy."

Agatha turned away from the coop and joined her sister on the other side of the lawn, next to the greenhouse.

"Where do you keep the pumpkins?"

Agatha shot her sister a knowing smile. "In here."

Fi leaned so close to the glass that her breath steamed on the greenhouse pane. "I can't see anything."

"Of course not. I didn't take any chances this year, I've concealed it." Agatha's lips curved up with self-satisfaction. She moved her hand in an upwards sweeping motion and the cloaking spell fell away.

Fi gaped at the ginormous pumpkin squatting in the middle of the greenhouse. "That's…"

The wyrm on her shoulder hissed.

"Impressive, isn't it? Will it do for entrapping a monster?"

"Er…if anything it's a bit much, you know, too…much. Have you got anything smaller?"

"Nonsense, it's perfect. And if this doesn't entice the pumpkin pulping maniac out, nothing will. Come on. I have to cut it from the vine soon anyway. Just steady the stepladder for me." Agatha grabbed a hacksaw from the tool shed and climbed up the wobbly ladder. A few minutes later, the pumpkin stem was cut, and a red-faced Agatha made her way back down.

"Er, how are we going to get it out of the greenhouse?"

"Don't you worry about that. After last year, I had a dwarf engineer the walls, so it can be disassembled. Stand back." Agatha pressed a button, and the sides of the greenhouse came away from the roof, lowering like a secret base was about to emerge from below the suburban garden. "OK, now let's get this into the truck…"

With a flick of her wrist, the pumpkin levitated up two inches off the ground. Agatha strode around the side of the house and the huge pumpkin followed behind like an obedient puppy. At the truck, she concentrated, beads of sweat forming on her forehead as she raised the pumpkin up and then lowered it lovingly into the flatbed of her pick-up truck. She climbed into the driver's seat and gave the four-leaf clover charm hanging on the mirror a quick rub as her sister joined her in the cab.

"There, all good. Let's go."

Chapter 32

"So where are we going?"

Fi brought up the map on her phone screen. "Omen Woods."

Agatha frowned. "And what do you think it is?"

"No idea."

"You must have some idea…I want to know if I'll need to bring my secateurs."

Fi rolled her eyes. "I think it's best for everyone if you leave them in the car."

"But–"

"I'm the agent here. Leave the bloody things in the car or you can't come with me."

Agatha stuck out her bottom lip and mumbled to herself as she drove.

*You made the right decision.*

"I know." Fi turned up the radio to tune out her sister's grumbles. The car moved quickly along the High Street and out of town towards the dark woods that lay beyond the crest of the small hill. Tendrils of mist snaked their way along the road, hiding the rolling fields from view. The fog thickened and even the car's fog lights couldn't penetrate the thick cloud.

Agatha slowed the vehicle and both sisters were silent as the car crawled toward the forest with eighties pop songs providing an eerie soundtrack to the strange journey.

Agatha pulled into the car park and braked hard, sending Fi jolting forward in her seat. Fi ignored her sister's petulant behaviour and climbed out, slamming the car door hard behind her. The fog muffled the sound, depriving her of the satisfaction of a loud bang, but, if there was a creature lurking in these woods then maybe quiet was better.

*Planning on sneaking up on it, are you?*

Fi scowled at the wyrm. "I know what I'm doing."

*Of course you do.* Cressida didn't sound like she believed the witch.

"Where do you want this, then?" Agatha unclipped the tailgate and stood looking up at the enormous pumpkin. Beads of mist condensed against its hard skin, as if the fog wanted to consume it. Fi rubbed her arms, maybe she should have waited until tomorrow morning to attempt to catch a monster, but she couldn't back out now and lose face in front of her sister. She'd never live it down, after all the times her sister had been in charge and bossed her about to 'help' her, Fi wasn't going to give up now she had all the authority of the Magical Liaison Office behind her.

"Just inside the woods should do it, on the path."

Agatha concentrated and levitated the massive vegetable over the dirt car park towards the entrance to the dark woods. The sisters slowed as they crossed the first tree.

"Is here OK?" Agatha whispered.

"That'll do," Fi agreed, instinctively lowering her voice in the thick fog.

Agatha placed the pumpkin carefully, but it still landed with a small bump. She winced and made to go and check on it.

"Leave it, we have to get into hiding."

Agatha bit her lip, but she nodded and followed Fi to a large bush on the other side of the path. "What do we do now?"

"Now, we wait."

# Chapter 33

They crouched behind the bush, peeping out between the dense cover of the leaves and waited. The last remnants of light faded, engulfed by the thick mist and the pair of witches shifted to ease cramps in their legs. Fi huffed out a breath and stood.

"Sorry Aggy, looks like I was wrong. Let's get out of here before it gets any colder."

Agatha eased herself upright and rubbed her arms to get some warmth back into them. Fi took a step towards the car park and paused as they heard the first rustle. Agatha pulled her sister back behind the bush and leaned forward, pushing apart the leaves so she could see better. Fi fell backwards on the damp ground, sending Cressida flying onto the floor. The wyrm hissed her displeasure and both sisters hushed the small animal. Fi twisted onto her front and froze.

From her position, she had a clear view between the bush's stubby branches. Something slithered over the leaves like a whisper. The deep fog muffled the sound and Fi frowned, trying to pinpoint the direction of the noise, but it was impossible. The crackle of leaves grew louder until it surrounded them and then a dark shape passed in front of the bush.

It was huge. That was all Fi could make out in the fog. It shifted like a shadow and paused in front of the huge pumpkin.

"Now?" mouthed Agatha, nudging Fi to get her attention.

Fi shook her head and motioned that they should wait. She wanted to find out more and the only way to do that was to follow the creature. She winced as a long tentacle snapped past them, then the thing slipped away into the cloud.

Fi counted to ten under her breath and pressed herself up from the floor.

"Are you alright, Cress?" she whispered.

*How many times must I tell you to stop calling me that?*

Cressida slunk over the ground and climbed up Fi's leg, digging her claws in through the witch's leggings.

"Is she OK?"

"She's fine."

They stepped out from behind their hiding place and hurried over to the empty spot where Agatha's prize pumpkin had stood moments before.

"Whatever it is, it must be strong." Agatha broke the silence.

Fi nodded and walked around the path; her eyes focused on the ground as she angled her phone's torch like a searchlight. "Did you see its tentacles?"

Her sister shuddered. "It looked like it had a lot of suckers too. What do you think it is?"

"No idea, but it went that way, and these tracks match the ones I saw at Harris' farm."

They peered down the footpath, straining their eyes as if that would help them penetrate the cold fog.

"Should we get some help?"

Fi shook her head. "Let's find out where it lives, and then we can call in some back up when we know what we're dealing with."

"And my pumpkin?"

Fi took a deep breath and forced herself to be calm. Her sister had offered to help and had sacrificed her pumpkin for the cause. "OK, we'll do some reconnaissance, rescue your pumpkin and go back and get help."

Fi's phone rang. "Hello?" she whispered, the unsettling mist making her cautious.

"Fi, thank goddess you answered. It's Cirian. I can't find him anywhere."

"Effie, calm down. He said he wanted to meditate."

"I know, but he's not in the garden and he's not answering his phone."

"OK. I'm kind of in the middle of something."

"I know, but I think he went to the woods after he spoke to you, and I have this feeling…"

The hairs on Fi's arms pricked up. Effie was psychic and it paid to listen to her feelings. "Omen Woods?"

“Yes.”

“I’m here now. Stay at home. I’ll find him.” Fi hung up, switched her phone to silent, and turned to Agatha. “OK, we find Cirian and your pumpkin and then get help.”

“Sounds like a plan.”

# Chapter 34

As they walked further into the murky woods, Agatha pulled her fleece-lined cagoule closer and Fi's eyes darted around, eyeing the skeletal trees for any sign of movement.

"Is there a part of this plan where we get murdered, and our bodies are never found?" Agatha whispered, her eyes skittering as she tried to make out shapes in the thick, grey fog.

"That's definitely not part of the plan."

"Good, good. Just checking." Agatha had her own phone out now and quickly shared her location with Neville. "Just a safety precaution," she muttered as Fi arched an eyebrow at her.

Fi nodded and they crept onwards, picking their way along the overgrown path, stepping over broken barbed wire fencing that looped along the ground.

"You're going to trip over that shoelace if you don't tie it up."

Fi glanced down at her feet, where one of the laces on her converse trainers trailed to one side. She bent down and jumped as a wild, brown rabbit ran across the path in a flurry of leaves. Cressida's tongue flicked out as the small animal disappeared into the undergrowth.

*I can smell pumpkins.*

"We're getting close," Fi said, keeping her voice low. She tucked the stray shoelace into the top of the trainer to save time and stood, her eyes darting around the woods. She stepped forward and tripped on a tree root, landing face first in something sticky.

Cressida yelped as she tumbled from Fi's shoulders for a second time and Fi fought to keep from throwing up as the overwhelming smell of rot filled her nostrils and mouth. She screwed her eyes shut; had she fallen into a bloated corpse?

Fi's mind filled with images of pink gore and exposed bones and bile burned up her throat. A firm hand grabbed her shirt and yanked her upright.

"What's the matter? It's only a pumpkin."

Fi latched onto Agatha's voice. Only a pumpkin, just a rotting vegetable that someone had left in the woods for the wildlife. She wiped her face with her sleeve, smearing orange pumpkin guts on her coat and opened her eyes. Yep, it was just a smashed pumpkin, nothing more. A hollow laugh escaped her mouth and she grinned sheepishly at her sister, but Agatha wasn't looking at her.

Fi followed her sister's gaze as the mist parted to give them a clear view of the clearing. Row after row of pumpkins in various states of mouldy decay were piled into every available space. Some had faces carved in them, looking over the woods from their perches, nestled into the crooks of tree branches or placed onto rotting logs filled with bright fungus.

It was a pumpkin graveyard. In the thick silence, a pumpkin fell from an ash tree with a sloppy splatter.

"Oh goddess, is that what I think it is?" Fi turned green as she spotted the purpling heads with glazed eyes sitting on either side of the largest tree. One of them had a candle stuck in its hair, burning faintly in the crowding fog and the other had large chunks rent from its cheeks, where maggots weaved in among the flesh.

Fi gathered her magic to her palms; there was a murderer somewhere in the trees.

"There!"

Fi whirled round, building her power into a ball of electricity. "Where? What did you see?" Her nerves tingled as adrenaline spiked through her body.

Agatha pointed to the largest pumpkin, resting in pride of place in the very centre of the clearing. "Let's grab my pumpkin and go find the popstar." She took a step forward, her face a strange shade of grey.

Fi reigned in her power and tugged Agatha's arm to stop her. "I need to see what took the pumpkins, leave it for a minute."

"I'm not risking my winning vegetable anymore! This is too dangerous. Let's go." Agatha raised her arms and the pumpkin levitated up a few inches off the ground. Fi held her breath as the huge vegetable moved towards them at a glacial pace.

A slithering noise followed by a loud thump filled the air. Fi looked past her sister to where a gigantic round shape rose up from across the clearing. Fi grabbed Agatha, pulled her backwards and ducked down behind a moss-covered log.

## Chapter 35

Fi's heart hammered against her chest, and she angled her phone to try to get some idea of what they were up against.

"What are you doing?" Agatha protested, wincing as her pumpkin hit the ground with a large thwack.

"Saving your neck. Any ideas, Cressida?"

The small wyrm shook her head from her spot near Fi's feet. *I can only sense your magic, normally I could taste magic from other beings, but all I can sense is pumpkin and the magic from you and Agatha.*

Fi abandoned the phone and stuck her head up to get a better view. She blinked. Long vines wrapped tenderly around Agatha's giant pumpkin, almost like they were caressing it and testing for bruises. For a second, Fi thought she was seeing double and then the creature came into focus.

"You're not going to believe this…" she whispered.

"What?" Agatha hissed and lifted herself to peek over the log. Her mouth fell open.

Standing over Agatha's prized pumpkin was another, even larger orange vegetable. Someone had graffitied its thick skin with a lopsided face, and it was moving around on large vines. Not tentacles, Fi thought, vines with leaves larger than her head.

Both witches stared.

"You don't think…"

Fi remembered Effie's veiled message to look to the past to solve the case. She swallowed hard. "I think that's your prize-winning pumpkin from last year."

The pumpkin had been in the back of the pick-up truck when the witches had confronted the murderous Margaret about killing Goody Winships at the previous Halloween Fete. It had ended in a showdown between the three and the fallout of magical energy had been enormous.

The vegetable had disappeared and while Fi and Agatha had thought it had been destroyed, there were theories that the combination of electrical and natural magic had brought it to life. It looked like those theories were true.

Fi cursed to herself. She'd had reports of a giant pumpkin roaming the Cotswolds, but she'd ignored them. They sounded like prank calls, and even if they were real, what damage could a pumpkin do?

Her eyes drifted to the two heads by the tree trunk, pulled by some grisly magnetic force, because it turned out that a pumpkin could kill, and it was her fault that these men were dead and their heads taken as some weird trophy or, the thought came into her mind, like a human jack o'lantern.

The blame froze her in place, staring into dead, glazed eyes that seemed to demand something of her that she couldn't give.

"Fi... Fi! Look."

Fi pulled herself out of her spiralling self-blame and forced her attention back to the pumpkin. "What's it doing?"

*I can sense elf magic.*

"It's got Cirian." Agatha frowned. "It looks like it's checking if the other pumpkin is OK. You don't think it's…caring for them, do you?"

Fi made a face. That was absurd, wasn't it?

A strange sad wailing made her look up and pause; was it crooning to the pumpkins?

Fi shook her head. It had murdered two people and she had to end it now. She should have pursued the reports earlier, but now she could correct her mistake and take this evil vegetable out.

"I told you, I can't heal pumpkins. My magic only works on living things," Cirian said in a tight voice.

The huge pumpkin whacked him across the back of his head with a spiky leaf, sending him sprawling to the ground.

Fi sent off a speedy text to the detective asking for back up, squared her shoulders, inhaled deeply, and fought off the retching feeling that flooded her as the mouldy smell of decomposing pumpkins hit her. She stood and stepped out from her hiding place.

She had to end this.

"Hey Pumpkin Head!" The sideways face turned to face her, and Fi looked it straight in its mismatched eyes. "You're under arrest."

Chapter 36

The pumpkin propelled itself forward with its thick vines, its huge unblinking graffiti eye seeming to focus on the witch. Fi drew her magic to her hands and took up a fighting stance.

"Motherrrr?"

Fi froze.

"Motherrr?" The voice was thick and deep, both squelchy and sonorous through the dense mist.

"Stay back." Fi motioned to Agatha and Cressida to stay behind the log.

"Pumpkin?" Agatha crept out from the log and stood next to Fi.

"Mother." Its voice was clear now.

"Of course, it isn't talking. It doesn't even have a mouth! It's a vegetable." Fi faltered as the pumpkin spoke again.

"I have waited for you."

"You're talking, aren't you?" Agatha sounded proud of the sentient vegetable.

"I am."

"Clever boy!"

"How?"

"I listened and learned."

*That explains everything.*

"OK, so you can talk. Why did you kill those humans?"

A strange hissing growl came from the creature. "The humans that killed my brothers and sisters?" One vine gestured to the mouldy, sagging pumpkins in the clearing.

"Oh, you poor thing."

"They're pumpkins, Aggy. That's what they're for."

"That is what we are for? Breaking our bodies, mutilating us, and leaving us outside as trophies on display to rot."

Fi tensed as the pumpkin loomed over them.

"I have only done the same to the ones who tried to stop me from rescuing my kin."

It made sense, in a twisted sort of way. "But you murdered people, I have to take you in."

"Wait!" Agatha stepped forward, blocking Fi's path. "Tell us more, how did you get here?"

The pumpkin shrugged. "I awoke in a metal prison with low walls. Alone and afraid."

"Does it mean the truck?"

"That must have been awful. Where did you go?"

"I escaped and fled to shelter."

*It's the size of a small car.*

"And no one saw you?"

"I moved from woods to woods, fascinated by humans, watching them, trying to find somewhere I could be safe."

"Of course, you want a home. I wish you'd stayed in the truck, I would have given you space in my garden. You'd love it. The soil is good, and I've got this special blend of compost…"

"Aggy. Not the time. What happened next?"

"Humans screamed at me and ran from me. I fled. I woke to others painting my skin with this," a leaf motioned to its strange spraypainted face. Close up, Fi saw a cracked piece of its orange skin moved in time with its speech, just off its black graffiti mouth. "I stayed away, watching, learning, listening, waiting."

"On your own this whole time, you poor thing."

"And then autumn came around. I saw my brothers and sisters in the fields."

"You wanted company." Agatha moved to pat its thick vine.

The huge pumpkin nodded. "I did. In the darker nights, I grew bolder and strayed closer to human dwellings and I learned their secret; that they massacre my kin and display us for fun."

"Not for fun, it's…tradition."

"Tradition." It spat out the word. "Dismembering and humiliating the corpses of my family."

"When you put it like that…" Fi shifted her feet, uneasy at the accusation.

"But, that was when I realised my purpose, I realised what I had been created for. What you created me for."

"Do you recognise my voice from when I sang to you in the greenhouse? Is that why you call me mother?"

"Alas, I cannot recall anything before I woke, but I recognise the magic that feeds me. Your magic."

"Didn't you grow it to win the largest vegetable prize?"

Agatha shot Fi a look. "I grew you to be as big as you could get and I'm so proud you've survived this long."

"Thank you, mother. And I vowed I would save as many others as I could and protect them with a hope of giving them life and having my own family."

Fi glanced around. Cressida pressed against her legs. A rustle sounded in the bushes.

*How many more living nightmare pumpkins are there?*

"But the magic that animates me does not transfer to those I wished to save. I had hoped the elf could help. When he wandered into my woods, it seemed like an answer to my prayers."

Fi glanced at Cirian, now propping himself up in the mud.

"But his magic does not work."

"So, you don't need him. You can let him go," Fi said, leaping on the chance to get Cirian out of harm's way.

"Anything for you, mother." The pumpkin nodded to the elf.

"Go on, go," Fi said to Cirian, hoping her voice was more confident than she felt.

He scrambled to his feet. "I'll get help."

"Just go!"

The elf ran, his shoes slipping on the wet ground.

"I am glad both of my parents are here." The pumpkin's face became more sinister as it raised itself up on its vines, so the sisters had to crane their necks upwards. "You will help me bring them to life."

Agatha and Fi stared around the ghoulish pumpkin display. "I don't think it works like that."

"No way."

*I knew there was a reason I didn't like vegetables.*

"But you made me. You can make others."

"Well, see, we didn't realise we'd made you, but maybe we could try…" Agatha looked at Fi, her blue eyes large and pleading.

"Really? You want to make more Frankenstein pumpkins? Even if we could, I'm not using my magic to create a monster."

"But you always say you want your magic to be more creative and less destructive. Please."

"You're being ridiculous. It was an accident from a magical overload, and–"

"An accident?" the pumpkin roared. "My creators think I am an accident? Made on a whim and discarded to rot?"

"No, it's not like that…"

"You will help me."

Agatha reached a hand out to the pumpkin. "There, there, pet, we want to help, we really do, but there's nothing we can do."

"If you are not with me, then you are against me."

"Aggy, watch out!"

The pumpkin lashed out with a thick vine and swatted Agatha away. She hit a tree hard and slumped to the ground.

Fi launched a blast of electricity at the monster. It dodged and a pumpkin behind it exploded in a mouldy splat. The creature slithered away into the depths of the wood with a low growl.

# Chapter 37

Fi took a step after it then stopped and ran to her sister. She bent down. "Aggy, are you alright?"

Agatha groaned, took Fi's proffered hand, and staggered to her feet, holding her back. "I'm alive, if that's what you mean."

"We have to stop it."

Agatha nodded grimly.

"Are you up for it?"

"Let's just find it."

Fi squeezed her sister's hand and pointed in the direction the pumpkin had gone. Ominous rustling sounded behind them, echoing through the trees.

Fi spun and loosed a blast of electricity. The blue-ish white light disappeared into the fog and crackled as it hit something. The witches squinted as a tendril of mist pulled back and revealed a scorched tree.

Fi swore softly and turned back. Beside her, Agatha's hands glowed green as she gathered her own nature magic.

A human head flew through the air towards Fi. It hit her square in the chest with a meaty thud.

Agatha screamed.

Fi stared with horror at the decapitated head in her hands. Its dark lips were pulled back, bearing yellowed teeth. Maggots crawled under the skin as if it were possessed.

Fi let out a cry and threw it away from her. It landed with a sharp crack on the earth, a gory mess seeping out onto the ground.

Agatha stumbled to a tree and bent over to heave out the contents of her stomach into a patch of decomposing pumpkins.

Fi wiped her hands on her coat, adding reddish stains to brown, and squinted into the fog. A second later, she was on her back.

The pumpkin had used the distraction to twine one of its snaking vines around her foot and now it pulled her along the forest floor, kicking and twisting as she tried to break free. Heedless of her comfort, it dragged her over tree roots and logs. She cursed her tightly tied converse trainers as she tried to shake free of its leafy grip.

Cressida darted along beside the vine in a flash of gold, breathing out fire to try to free the witch. Fi swore as an errant flame licked along her calf. "Watch where you're breathing! I'm not fireproof."

*Be more grateful. I'm saving your life.*

A straggling shoelace worked itself free. Fi concentrated and used her other foot to lever off the slightly looser trainer. It came free and took her stripy sock with it. Fi scrambled to her feet, panting as she twisted around, seeking out the monster.

She moved backwards slowly, hands up in front of her, magic primed. Movement caught her eye, and she released a blast of electricity.

"Watch where you're magicking!" Agatha emerged from the mist, her breath coming in small clouds in the chill of the early night.

"Sorry. Be careful, it's around here somewhere." Fi shuffled backwards and slammed into something hard.

"Fi." There was a note of warning in Agatha's voice.

The tech witch swallowed. "It's behind me, isn't it."

"Duck!"

Fi dived out of the way as Agatha blasted it with her own nature magic. The pumpkin glowed an eerie emerald green for a split second, then it shuddered and sank to the ground.

"Great job, Aggy," Fi said, pushing herself upright.

Agatha gaped at a spot behind Fi's shoulder. Fi turned slowly and saw the pulsing pumpkin grow larger and larger, the painted face growing with it.

"Fudge it," Agatha swore.

"What the hell?!"

"I'm not used to destroying plants, my magic must be feeding it!"

"Just run!"

Fi and Agatha fled as the gigantic pumpkin towered over them. It thrashed out with a vine the same thickness as Fi's leg and knocked Agatha to one side. "Aggy!"

Fi leapt over a vine and scrambled to her sister. A leaf wrapped around her stomach and yanked the tech witch away. Another vine snaked over to Agatha.

The nature witch pulled the secateurs from her coat pocket and hacked at the creature. It flailed and yanked the tool from her hands, leaving her defenceless.

"Cressida, help Agatha!" Fi yelled, struggling to free herself from the fuzzy leaf.

# Chapter 38

Fi ripped through the leaf with her bare hands, wrenching the green flesh in two and wincing at the spikes that pierced her skin.

The pumpkin dropped her with a hiss.

She hit the ground hard and cried out as her bare foot landed on a rock. With a strange hopping run, she hurried to the nearest tree and leaned against it. The cold air hit the back of her lungs as she panted hard.

Thick silence fell over the forest. A burst of flaming orange light to the left showed where Cressida protected Agatha, but where was the killer pumpkin?

The mist parted and Fi launched a blast of electricity at a large shape. A log exploded in a shower of splinters and fungus. And she'd just given away her position.

She hobbled forward, the electricity tingling under her skin distracting her mind from the pain in her hands and foot. Vines twisted round her, pinning her arms to her sides. The pumpkin loomed out of the mist. A vision of mottled orange and that creepy graffitied face, straight out of some Halloween film.

"So, will you help me now, mother?"

Fi gritted her teeth. "I can't bring things to life. That's not how my magic works."

"It worked with me."

"You want to see what I can do?" Fi concentrated on the magic that bubbled inside her. Instead of drawing it to her palms in a focused ball, she envisioned the electricity seeping from her pores and surrounding her in a shield of energy. Blue light swirled around the witch, sparking as her magic obeyed her.

She pushed it outwards, expanding her shield. The vines sizzled and retreated.

"Mother." The pumpkin turned its face to her, it almost looked like she'd betrayed it.

Fi shook her head. Nonsense. It was a vegetable.

It snapped out with its vines.

Fi jumped, then ducked and slid as she avoided the solid whips. The pair of secateurs whizzed past Fi's head as the frenzied flailing dislodged the tool.

Fi cursed. She had told Agatha to leave the blasted things in the car.

The vines thrashed over and over.

She weaved through them, but she was slowing down. One caught the back of her knee, and she sank to the ground with a cry.

She rolled to the side as a huge vine crashed into the mud where she had lain. She crawled backwards in a strange crabwalk as she tried to get out of range.

The pumpkin raised its vines once more and cracked them down. Fi closed her eyes and pushed her magic out in a pulse.

Chapter 39

The sickly, smoky smell of green wood burning filled Fi's nostrils and she covered her mouth with one muddy, bleeding palm. She opened her eyes. The pumpkin sank back to the opposite side of the small clearing, shaking its blackened vines.

Fi rolled over and forced herself to her feet with a grunt. She faced the monster, her chest heaving with exertion. The witch stepped forward and the creature shrunk away.

"Wait!"

Fi turned to Agatha, her heart pounding against her chest. "Out of the way, Aggy."

"You can't kill it, you're its mother. With me. We're both mothers. He's our baby." Agatha planted herself between the huge pumpkin and Fi.

*That is one big baby.*

"Aggy." Fi's voice was low with warning.

"Please."

"Agatha." Fi hardened her voice.

Agatha swallowed and moved aside, her bottom lip wobbling in the dim light.

Fi gathered her power to her palms. They glowed with an electric blue light. This was why she shouldn't have kids, her power only brought pain, even when paired with her sister's nature magic that promoted growth, she had managed to create a monster.

She glanced at Agatha's pleading face and then to the twisted dark graffiti that was the pumpkin's face. Her power was destruction and deep in her heart, she knew she could kill it. She imagined the thick skin smouldering under her magical blast and wet pulp spraying across the trees.

But this thing, whatever it was, was alive. And it wasn't attacking her. Not anymore.

Its vines trailed limply on the mulch of the forest floor. Fi gazed into the misshapen painted eyes, it looked…sad. Fi screwed her face up, undecided.

*You don't have to do this.*

Fi's eyes snapped down to the familiar at her feet. "What else can I do? I can't let it go."

*You always have a choice.* Cressida jerked her head to the barbed wire winding through the leaves.

Behind her, Fi heard the tramp of footsteps as back-up arrived. If she didn't kill it, they would.

She drew more magic to her hands. The footsteps stopped and she heard guns cock.

"Bloody hell," someone said.

Fi made her choice. "Stand back, I've got this."

She raised her hand. Agatha turned away, unable to watch. Fi took a breath and released her power into the barbed wire.

The electrified fence buzzed as it came alive, creating a barrier between the pumpkin and the police. The scent of cooked pumpkin filled the air and Fi looked around, puzzled, before the inanimate prize-winning pumpkin from Agatha's greenhouse exploded in a pulpy bang, coating the woods in a smattering of pips and pumpkin flesh.

It was almost artistic, like Japanese anime in a watery orange. Fi grinned as the pulp splattered across her face. No one was hurt, except for a vegetable. A real vegetable, not the strange living thing that still whimpered in the small clearing.

Agatha stared in horror at the mess and her eyes filled with tears. "The Halloween Fete…my prize…"

Neville burst through the trees, his chest heaving. He brandished a can of pepper spray, his eyes wild until they rested on Agatha. "Darling, are you alright?"

Agatha frowned at her husband. "Where's Bea?"

"With your mum. Are you hurt?"

A loud voice shouted across the woods. "Why are there civilians here?" A harpy pushed her way through the armed police officers, glaring at any that met her eye. Her task force followed, carving a path through the mundane police.

Her gaze lit on Fi. "Fiona."

"Gwendolyn," Fi greeted the familiar harpy with a nod.

“What the hell happened here?”

177

# Chapter 40

Fi awoke the next morning with a groan and pulled the covers back over her head. It had been a long night. She had powered the fence for hours while the Magical Liaison Office containment unit argued over the best way to imprison the pumpkin. The harpy in charge had not been pleased by the night-time call out and had let everyone know about it.

Eventually, they had decided to transport it to a dedicated area of the Breconian reserve, a sort of nature preserve that housed all sorts of magical creatures.

It had taken hours to get the wards in place, but they had confirmed it would be a suitable prison in the early hours of the morning. The pumpkin wouldn't hurt anyone else and could live out its life in peace, tending a pumpkin patch of its own.

Agatha worried that the pumpkin might get bullied by manticores and, of course, Breconia was home to dragons as well…the thought of the sentient pumpkin being roasted had almost driven her sister to tears.

Agatha had mentioned containing it in their garden was an option, but Fi had persuaded her that Breconia was the best place for it.

The only place, if they didn't want to humanely end the pumpkin right there, because there was no way they could allow it to roam free in the Cotswolds after it had killed two people. And confining it to Agatha's greenhouse wasn't a practical solution.

Besides, dragons ate meat, not pumpkins.

Neville had joined in on Fi's side. He had helped convince Agatha with a tactical mention of the danger to their daughter, before leading her away to collect Bea from the Bed & Breakfast, where Nell was looking after her granddaughter.

Fi couldn't help the small smile that crept over her face as she recalled Neville's entrance onto the scene as an unlikely hero; what was he going to do? Interpret tax regulation at an assailant.

*What are you laughing about?*

Fi reached out and stroked the blinking wyrm. "Neville showing up last night." She shook her head.

*You shouldn't laugh. He was courageous. With no idea what he'd find, he went out into the night to save his wife from whatever dangerous situation he had conjured in his mind. You should be happy your sister has such a protector.*

"Yeah, maybe. Since when did you become so lyrical?"

A knock on the door interrupted the conversation. "Come in."

Effie entered with a spring in her step. "Congratulations on cracking the case. I knew you could do it."

"How do you know I solved it?"

"Cirian told me what happened." She smiled down at the tech witch. "And now that's out of the way, we can focus on the grand re-opening and the concert."

"Steve's got it under control." Fi muffled a yawn.

"Naturally, but that doesn't mean he couldn't use some help. I'm heading over after breakfast." The older witch in a younger body waited.

"Fine. I'll come too."

A shower and a clean change of clothes later, Fi was downstairs helping herself to a pot of strong Goblin Blend coffee and toast. "Where's Cirian?"

"He likes to commune with nature before he performs. He's in the garden."

Fi glanced out of the window to see the elf seated cross-legged beneath a Japanese maple tree wearing a greenish grey tunic. Red star-shaped leaves drifted gently to the ground with every small breath of a breeze. The garden was a much better choice than the woods he'd walked to last night.

Timaeus eyed the intruder but decided he wasn't worth the effort of moving across the lawn to annoy or attack.

"Ready?" asked Effie.

The younger witch nodded, and they headed to the café with Cressida in tow.

"One thing I don't miss about my old body is the aches and pains, you have no idea how good it feels just to be able to move freely again."

# Chapter 41

"You don't like me, and I don't like you, but my friend, Steve, has got a café to open and so help me, the customers are going to get freshly ground coffee from your stupid jets or I will personally take you down to the dump and see to it that you are put in the stinkiest, most disgusting part of the tip that I can find. Do I make myself clear?"

The coffee machine didn't move. Fi took that as a yes.

Steve hovered by the nearest table, folding and refolding a napkin into an origami swan. Effie had chased him away from rearranging the gemstone display by size for the tenth time and sat in the back room, communing with her new crystal ball, or possibly taking a nap. Fi wasn't sure. She ignored Steve's gaze as his eyes flitted from her to the napkin.

"OK then, let's get you started up."

She plugged in the machine and pressed the on button, then the reset button, hidden behind a small panel at the back. The machine started with a click and a soft whirr then went silent.

Cressida lifted her head from her spot in the corner at the noise.

So far, so good. She tipped some beans into the grinder and pressed another button. A smile curved her lips as the beans became a fine powder and the rich aroma of coffee wafted over the café with an accompanying purr from the machine. She gave it a pat.

"Now for the real test." She transferred the powder to the sump and tamped it down, relishing the strong smell of freshly ground coffee. With a practised click and twist, she attached the sump to the machine and placed two mugs underneath it. Another button and the Bellissimo Coffee 2000 ramped up to a growl, before releasing boiling brown water into the mugs with a satisfying hiss.

Fi waited for the stream of liquid to finish before removing a mug and inhaling deeply, it smelled good. She sipped it carefully. Goodness, it tasted good too.

"And one last test Bella…" Fi poured milk into a metal jug and angled it under the steam jet. With a twist, she released the scalding hot steam into the milk and jiggled the jug, so the white liquid transformed into frothy foam. She stopped the steam and the machine's hissing petered out. She poured the foamy milk into the second mug and sprinkled chocolate powder on top.

"And we have coffee," she announced.

Steve clapped excitedly and grabbed his cup so hard, some of his cappuccino slopped to the floor. He blew on it then drank. The werewolf's eyes closed in pleasure. "Delicious," he proclaimed.

They were all set for the grand opening.

# Chapter 42

"Another latte, please."

Fi rolled her shoulders and fiddled with the coffee machine, which, aside from a couple of random spurts of steam, was working perfectly. Steve and Fi had discovered a natural rhythm where the werewolf took orders and sorted the cakes while Fi made the drinks. She sneaked a look at the counter. The batch of scones she had made were nearly gone and Steve's oversized Victoria sponge was down to its last slice.

The café was packed full of eager patrons. Fi wanted to think it was because of the treats on offer or the eclectic atmosphere but they were mostly here to get a glimpse of Cirian, the famous elven popstar. A microphone stood at the back of the café, between the shelves of trinkets and crystals for sale.

"I'm going to check on Effie, she's meant to be making a speech. Can you take care of orders for a minute?"

Fi nodded. There was a break between customers, and she busied herself by wiping down the temperamental machine.

"Can I get one of the best scones in the Cotswolds, please?"

Fi turned at the familiar voice. Mort smiled at her.

"I don't know if they're the best…but they're pretty good." She scooped one off the display stand and placed it onto a small china plate with a miniature pot of jam and tub of cream. "Anything else?"

"I'll have a latte please, and a date, if it's still on offer."

"I didn't see that on the menu," Fi said, tapping her chin and pretending to think.

"That's alright, I'll just stand at the counter, and we can pretend we're having coffee together."

She snorted a laugh. "Romantic."

His lips quirked and Fi's heart both jumped and melted into a puddle all at once. Her voice was breathy when she said, "I choose the activity?"

He bowed his head. "Naturally."

"Then it's a date." She turned and grinned at the coffee machine as she made the latte, using the foam to make a heart shape on top of the drink. Fi frowned. It looked more like a bottom than a heart. She sprinkled a hefty helping of chocolate powder over the top to hide the messy foam. A coffee artist she was not.

"And what about tonight?" Mort asked.

"Tonight?" Fi stared at him blankly.

"The concert. Are you going with anyone?"

It was sweet that he thought he had competition, when the truth was, she hadn't had any male interest since her ex.

Unless you counted her fellow agent, Maxi, who had been more interested in her powers than her personality.

"No. You?" Fi held her breath as she waited for his reply.

"Well, there was someone I was hoping to go with…" Fi felt her heart sink down past her feet, through the foundations of the coffee shop and lodge itself somewhere deep underground. The doctor was tall, dark and handsome, of course he had women waiting in line to go on dates with him. "But I'm not sure if she wants to go with me, she's not very good at saying what she's feeling sometimes…"

*He means you, you idiot.* Cressida spoke from the corner where she had curled up out of the way of the 'horde' as she named the paying customers.

"Oh. Oh! Right. Well, I'm sure she'd love to go with you…if you asked her."

Mort's eyes crinkled as he smiled down at her. "Would you like to go to the concert with me?"

Fi nodded.

"I'll wait for you to finish up here."

Fi smiled at him, then turned to serve the next customer as he found his way to the quiet corner by Cressida. If the café stayed this busy, they'd have to get a takeaway window outside.

Steve ducked back behind the counter to help, and Effie glided towards the microphone, with a knowing smile. She nodded at Fi, and the tech witch dimmed the lights, leaving a single spotlight on the young nonagenarian. Her sequinned dress twinkled under the light and her hair cascaded down her back in shimmery waves. Fi's hand went to her own white hair, back in its usual ponytail and frizzy as ever after using so much power the other night. She needed some more of that elven conditioner. The lights flickered and Fi forced herself to concentrate on keeping the spotlight on.

"As many of you know, a great calamity happened here. A fire destroyed this humble café and killed me…I mean, my aunt." Fi shook her head. Great recovery Effie.

Very few people knew about the transfer of souls that had placed the elderly witch into the young body she now inhabited, and they'd agreed it was best to keep it that way.

So, Effie had taken up the life of the young woman, although she kept her own name. "After a lot of hard work, most of it from the lovely Steve, ably assisted by Fiona…" She gestured to the two people standing behind the counter and both Fi and Steve gave a small wave to the crowd. "I'm so pleased we have been able to reopen today, just in time for Halloween."

A smattering of polite applause filled the café and Effie nodded regally. "Now, I understand it's tradition for someone to cut a ribbon, so I have asked my good friend, Cirian, who you may have heard of…" A ripple of laughter ran through the crowd. "…to cut this ribbon. Fi, Steve, if you would be so kind."

Fi grabbed the red ribbon from the shelf underneath the till and squeezed through the people to reach Effie. She stood next to the display of skulls while Steve held the other end of the sparkly ribbon on the opposite side of the room. Cirian stepped out from the back room, looking elegant and attractive in his rockstar clothing, that would have made anyone else look like a poser. He beamed around the room as if he couldn't imagine being anywhere else and ran a hand through his artfully mussed hair.

The elf took the scissors and paused for photos as everyone pulled out their smartphones. The photographer from the local paper knelt at the front of the table, taking angled shots. Sita whooped from her seat.

Cirian cut the ribbon slowly, and with flair before flashing Effie a special smile and moving to stand beside her for more photos. The woman actually blushed. Fi didn't think she'd ever seen the older witch embarrassed before.

"Thank you, Cirian." The crowd cheered again. Someone shouted out that they loved him, and his smile became strained. "And now, I expect you want to hear this gorgeous elf sing."

The whoops were louder this time and Effie held up her hands to motion for quiet.

"Of course, it wouldn't be fair to everyone waiting outside to have the performance in here, so if you head to the common, Cirian will perform at six o'clock this evening."

More cheers and the elf bowed and waved before heading into the back room tucking Effie's hand into the crook of his arm as they left.

"Should I go after them?" asked Steve.

Fi shook her head. "I wouldn't. Best to leave them alone." She'd caught the looks that the elf had shot the witch and didn't think they wanted to be disturbed.

The customers drank up and began to leave now that the celebrity had disappeared. Fi's mother strode over and placed her empty cup on the counter. Agatha and her family trailed behind.

"Good job, both of you."

Fi blinked and then her mouth curved into a surprised smile at the rare praise from her mother.

"Yes, well done Steve, and Fi." Agatha grinned at them. "Glad you got everything sorted in time."

"Thanks, it was a shame about the pumpkins, but great idea of Fi's to make the display less obvious."

"Well, I'm not sure that witches' hats are less obvious…"

"Just take the compliment."

Fi shut her mouth.

"Now, I've got to get to the common to make sure everything's ready for the concert." Nell said. "Get there early if you want to get a good spot and remember your tickets." She swept out of the room.

Fi and Agatha shared a private look about their bossy mother and then burst into giggles while the others looked on in bemusement.

# Chapter 43

Fi waited until the last stragglers had left before cleaning down the counter and the coffee machine for a final time. The sun dipped below the horizon as Steve placed the chairs upside down on the café tables.

"I think I'm going to leave off the tablecloths for day-to-day opening. Look at the stains on this." He held up a formerly white cloth with a smear of purple jam rubbed into it next to a yellowish mark.

"Good idea."

"We should talk shifts as well, now that Effie's back and I know you've got your MLO job, but at least tell me you'll keep making scones."

"Of course, I will, but can we talk about this tomorrow? Mort's waiting and…"

"Say no more. What are shift patterns in the face of true love?"

Fi sputtered, "I don't know about love…"

Steve smirked at her and tapped the side of his nose. "The nose never lies, Fi. I've got animal intuition about this sort of thing. Right, I think I'm done. Stand on the doormat while I sweep."

Fi obeyed, her face still a bright pink from Steve's love comment. The werewolf hummed as he worked, and the floor was soon free of crumbs.

"Effie, we're locking up," Fi called before stepping outside with Steve. Mort stood by the door, holding a wicker picnic basket with Cressida at his feat eyeing the basket as it swung overhead. Fi moved next to him and smiled as he placed his arm over her shoulders.

"Should we wait for them?" Steve asked, peering in past the closed sign.

Fi opened her mouth when she noticed the grey figure skulking against the wall. She frowned, trying to place the familiar face.

"There you are. I've been waiting for ages."

"Valentine! Good to see you, are you OK?"

"No, I'm not OK." His voice mocked hers.

"Take it easy, alright." Mort's gaze darkened. Fi placed a hand on his chest.

"It's alright. What happened?"

"Exactly what I said would happen. Someone found out I was a vampire and they set light to my house. Everything I had is gone and what am I supposed to do now? I had to escape during the daytime. Do you know how hard it is to run for your life while staying in the shade?"

Fi bit her lip to refrain from making things worse. The vampire's skin had a pinkish tinge.

"I can prescribe you a cream for the sunburn," Mort said.

Valentine glared at him. "And what about the rest. All my stuff's gone; I don't have anywhere to stay…"

"Aren't there any other vampires you can bunk with?"

He gave Fi a cold look. "None that will take me in. Our kind can be pretty snotty if you're under seventy. I was saving up to get to London, I hear there's a company owned by vampires there who'll take on supernaturals. But now I'm homeless!"

He stopped ranting as Effie and Cirian exited the shop. Effie's wavy hair was rumpled, and her lipstick was slightly smeared.

"What's all this?"

"Effie, this is Valentine. He's a vampire who's been burned out of his home."

"That's terrible! What are you going to do?"

Valentine kicked his feet miserably. "I don't know. I've got nowhere to go."

"Then you can stay here," Effie declared.

"Really?"

"Really?" Steve wrinkled his nose.

"Absolutely. We'll need the extra help, and you can sleep in the back room when you need to. I won't be using it much. Plus, having a vampire means we can expand our opening hours."

Steve gripped Effie's arm and half turned away from the group. "Are you sure?"

"Of course," she brushed him away and shot a sideways glance at the elf. "I'm thinking of going off travelling again so you'll need the help. You can't rely on Fi to take on any shifts, she's got an important job at the Magical Liaison Office." Effie turned back to the vampire. "But no snacking on the clientele or you'll be out on your ear young man."

"Vampire's honour." Valentine placed a sunburned hand over his chest and bowed.

"Well, we'd better do this properly, hadn't we? I, Ophelia Harrington, proprietor of this café do hereby welcome the vampire Valentine…"

"Lapell," the vampire supplied.

"…Lapell into this dwelling. Go on then." Effie held the door open, and the vampire stepped inside, surveying his new home.

"Thank you," he took her hand and shook it warmly, "you have no idea what this means to me. Thank you, a thousand times."

"Not at all. Now, we have a concert to attend. Steve, could you lock up?" With that, Effie linked her arm through Cirian's and they headed off to the common.

Steve eyed the vampire, his hazel eyes turning amber as his inner wolf came to the surface. "Put one foot wrong, vampire…"

Valentine held up his hand, rocking on his heels. "Got it. But you don't have to worry about me."

"Don't wreck my display," Steve growled as Valentine reached for a shelf of Tarot decks.

Fi took the keys from Steve before he bent them out of shape. "Er, did you want to file a report about the fire?"

Valentine tilted his head to one side. "Maybe…"

"OK, I'll come and take some details tomorrow." She turned the key in the lock and watched through the window as the vampire explored his new home.

"Don't mess up my clean floor!" Steve shouted through the glass.

Valentine smiled and jumped onto a table instead. The werewolf glared at him and bared his teeth.

"Come on, Steve, you don't want to miss the show. Glen will be waiting for you."

The mention of his partner cleared Steve's head and he allowed Fi to lead him away by the hand while Mort wrapped his arm around her shoulder again.

# Epilogue

They held out their tickets to the shimmering ward that spanned the common and walked through the barrier and to the gate that led onto the green. Others, dressed in the trademark sunshine yellow of Cirian's fans, tried to get through without a ticket and slammed into the ward with a thud and a shriek as they fell to the ground.

Fi raised an eyebrow, impressed with the magical protection on display. The local Witches', Wizards' and Warlocks' Institution had gone all out to protect the popstar. A familiar vampire in a yellow chunky knit jumper flashed her Magical Liaison Office badge at them along with her fangs. "Good to see you, Fi. Standard security check."

Fi got out her own badge and the vampire nodded acknowledgement but still held up the small, black oblong and waved her forward to be checked. She ran it over Fi's arms and legs like an airport security scanner, while Fi finally remembered the vampire's name.

"Hi Dot, I didn't realise you were coming."

A smile lit up Dot's pale face. "Are you joking? I've been trying to get on the security detail for a Cirian performance for years, so when this one came up, I jumped at the chance."

"Are you here with anyone else?" Fi craned her neck, looking for more MLO agents.

"No one else wanted to travel and Agent Jones was satisfied with the arrangements after she had a full briefing from your mother."

Fi nodded along like she knew that her mother had spoken to her boss.

Dot leaned forward. "She was on the phone for over three hours," she said meaningfully.

Fi groaned. She was going to have to speak to her mum about boundaries one day. Fi stepped forward and Dot scanned Mort and Steve.

"Thanks all, maybe see you later."

"Enjoy the concert," Fi said as they crossed the green and headed towards the stage.

Steve rushed off to find his partner and daughter, leaving Mort and Fi to pick a spot to sit.

"Any preferences?" Mort asked.

Fi tapped the side of her face, pretending to weigh up the options. "Well, we could sit on the ground."

Mort flashed her a smile and tugged her towards a spot to the right of the stage, near the trees. It was more secluded and apart from most of the concert goers, who had chosen to sit directly in front of the stage. Fi could see minor turf wars going on as people rearranged their picnic blankets and jostled for prime spots. She nodded; this spot was perfect.

Mort placed the wicker basket on the ground and dug out a blanket, which he tossed at Fi, while he found a thermos of something and two mugs.

Fi smoothed down the tartan blanket over the damp grass and sat. Mort joined her and offered her a mug. They clinked them together and Fi sipped the drink, enjoying the warming sensation of the mulled cider.

"Do you like it?"

"Mmmm."

"I brewed it myself."

"A man of many talents."

"You have no idea," he said, his voice deep and husky.

Fi took another drink, telling herself that the warm feeling spreading through her stomach was from the cider and not his words, full of promise. She paused. Why was she fighting these feelings?

*You're overthinking things.* Cressida yawned and curled up on the corner of the rug nearest the basket.

Fi pulled a face at her familiar and thought. She was always uncomfortable talking about her feelings and reading other people's emotions, that was part of the reason that she preferred the simplicity of interaction online. But, if she didn't allow herself to feel, she could lose everything that was starting with Mort, whatever that was.

And she didn't want that to happen.

She bit her lip, considering. He was waiting for her to lead, she was almost certain about that, so what was she waiting for?

She patted his leg and shifted until she was practically in his lap before leaning back against Mort's muscled chest. He wrapped his arms around her, his body heat warmed her through her jumper, cementing her decision. She swallowed, steeling herself to share her feelings.

"Mort," she whispered.

"Fi." His hot breath caressed her ear, sending a wave of heat through her body.

"I want to try and make this, whatever this is, work."

"So do I." He pulled her more tightly to him and planted a kiss on her neck. Fi shivered and then pulled away so she could face him. She had to look into his eyes.

"But I don't want any secrets between us. You know about me. I'm a witch with electrical powers that don't always work how I want and…I've hurt people…" Mort opened his mouth to speak, and Fi placed a finger on his lips.

"No, don't interrupt, I know what my magic does, what I've done, but I'm learning to control it better so I can protect rather than injure. I'm not great at sharing my feelings or sharing my heart. I love videogames and most of the time, I'd rather stay inside, but I want to spend time with you, and I really care for you, even if I don't show it all the time. So, I just thought you should know…" she trailed off.

"I do know. Thank you for sharing that with me. I don't want you to change." He leaned forward and kissed her, softly on the lips. Fi reached her arms around his neck and pulled herself closer, deepening the kiss. He broke away. "I want to be honest with you too."

Fi tucked a stray strand of hair behind her ear. This was it. The part where he admitted to having a wife and three kids hidden away in another country.

"I can't speak about my powers or my purpose, I don't know how, but I can show you. Whenever you're ready, but…I'm scared."

"Scared?" Fi's brow furrowed. What did he have to be scared of?

"I don't want to lose you and, when you learn about my world, I'm worried you'll run."

Fi thought for a long minute. "Mort." She tipped his chin up with her hand, forcing him to look at her. "I know what sort of person you are and nothing about your powers will change what I think about you. When you're ready to show me, I want to find out more about your world."

Mort kissed her again. "How about tonight?"

Around them, the seated crowd cheered as Cirian took to the stage.

"After the show." Fi smiled and turned so she was sat in his lap again and his arms pulled her close.

Cirian waved as he walked to the centre of the stage. He picked up the microphone and the crowd went wild. "Hello, Omensford!"

More cheers. He waited for them to settle down before performing an upbeat song about a girl he used to know.

"This next song goes out to an incredible witch, entrepreneur, and my good friend. Ladies and gentlemen, witches and warlocks, give it up for Effie!"

Everyone cheered as he descended the steps and made his way towards the witch seated with Nell on a starry blanket near the front. He pulled her up and crooned his way through a love ballad before kissing her hand and taking his place back on the stage for the rest of his set.

Fi sank back against Mort and allowed herself to enjoy this moment, because she had no idea what Mort had in store for her after the concert.

# Thank you

A special thank you to my amazing patrons: Emma Ward and Mark Canty who always supports me.

If you want to support Gemma, you can find her on www.patreon.com/G_Clatworthy for exclusive first reads of new stories.

You can also join her newsletter at www.gemmaclatworthy.com for a free prequel to her Rise of Dragons series and follow Gemma on www.instagram.com/gemmaclatworthy, www.facebook.com/gemmaclatworthy or join the Facebook reader's group Gemma's book wyrms.

# Other Books by G Clatworthy

Books in the Rise of the Dragons series:

Awakening

Solstice of Dragons

Equinox Betrayal

Darkest Deception

Attack on Avalon

Fated Bloodlines


Books in the Omensford series (set in the Rise of the
Dragons universe):

Bedsocks and Broomsticks

Cream Teas and Crystal Balls

Donkeys and Demons

Pumpkins and Popstars

Exes and Enchantments

# Children's Books

**The Child Who series:**

The Girl Who Lost Her Listening Ears

The Boy Who Lost His Listening Ears

The Girl Who Dreamed of Sleep

The Boy Who Dreamed of Sleep


**Nanny Pastry series:**

Nanny Pastry and the Nimble Ninjabread Man


**Other books:**

Coronavirus in the words of children

# About the Author

Gemma started writing during the 2020 lockdown and loves fantasy fiction and dragons in particular. She lives in Wiltshire with her family and two cats and also enjoys crafts of all kinds. You can see all her writing on www.patreon.com/G_Clatworthy. Join the conversation at Gemma's book wyrms readers' group on Facebook.

She also writes children's books. You can find out more on her website www.gemmaclatworthy.com or follow her on Instagram (www.instagram.com/gemmaclatworthy) or Facebook (www.facebook.com/gemmaclatworthy).